CAT IN THE CRYPT

'Bathsheba! Puss, puss, puss!' Mandy called.

There was no answering miaow; no sign of a big tabby cat. Mandy worked her way around the outside of the church, looking into each dark hollow and crevice where a cat might shelter.

James was calling out Bathsheba's name too, as he worked his way up and down the rows of headstones. His voice sounded lost and eerie in the empty churchyard.

Just then, as the moon slid behind a cloud, pitching the church and churchyard into deeper darkness, a streak of light seemed to dart past Mandy. She swallowed hard and turned her head. *What was that?*

Animal Ark series

LUCY DANIELS

Cat
– *in the* –
Crypt

Illustrations by Ann Baum

**Hodder
Children's
Books**

a division of Hodder Headline plc

Special thanks to Susan Bentley
Thanks also to C. J. Hall, B.Vet.Med., M.R.C.V.S., for reviewing
the veterinary information contained in this book.

Animal Ark is a trademark of Working Partners Ltd
Text copyright © 1999 Working Partners Ltd
Created by Working Partners Ltd, London W12 7QY
Illustrations copyright © 1999 Ann Baum
Original series created by Ben M. Baglio

First published in Great Britain in 1999
by Hodder Children's Books

A Catalogue record for this book is available from the British Library

ISBN 0 340 73601 1

Typeset by Avon Dataset Ltd, Bidford-on-Avon, Warks

Printed and bound in Great Britain by
Clays Ltd, St Ives plc

Hodder Children's Books
a division of Hodder Headline plc
338 Euston Road
London NW1 3BH

One

The wrought-iron gate of the crypt swung slowly open. Mandy Hope watched a pale, creamy-grey cat emerge from the darkness and pad up the steps into the church. Silently, it walked down the empty nave and slid out of the open front door. In the churchyard it paused to look around, its face in deep shadow. Then it laid back its ears and began to call; a strange haunting howl echoing round the graves . . .

Mandy jerked awake and sat bolt upright in bed. The dream was still there at the back of her mind, sending little chills prickling down her spine. Over the past two weeks, she'd had the exact same dream almost every night. She shivered and reached out to snap on the bedside light.

The familiar sights of her own room were comforting, but it was cold now that the central heating was off. She thought of snuggling back under the quilt, but felt wide awake. Maybe a hot drink would help her to get back to sleep.

In the kitchen she had just boiled a kettle and was spooning drinking chocolate into a mug when a voice behind her said, 'Is there enough hot water for two?'

'Oh!' Mandy spun round. 'Dad! I tried to be quiet.'

Adam Hope ruffled his daughter's shortish fair hair. 'That's all right, love. I was reading in bed, catching up on some articles in one of my vet's magazines. What woke you? Was it that dream again?'

Mandy nodded as she reached for another mug. 'It's weird, Dad. I mean – how come it's always the same? I'm sure the dream must mean something, but I haven't a clue what!'

Mr Hope sat at the kitchen table and propped

his chin on his hand. 'Hmm. I'm no expert at interpreting dreams, but I'd say something's definitely preying on your mind.'

Just then, Emily Hope came into the kitchen, looking sleepy-eyed. Her red hair was loose round her shoulders. 'Can anyone join the party?' she joked. 'I wouldn't want to miss anything.'

Mandy grinned at her mum. 'Hot chocolate times three, then!'

'I heard you talking about these dreams you've been having, love,' Mrs Hope said. 'I think they could have something to do with Bathsheba.'

Mandy blinked. Bathsheba was the big tabby cat who had belonged to old Reverend Madeley. The tabby had been a familiar sight in Walton Parish Church, which was used by Mandy's school for services at Christmas, Easter and Harvest Festival. Sadly, Reverend Madeley had died a couple of weeks ago and Bathsheba hadn't been seen since.

Mr Hope nodded thoughtfully. 'I think your mum may be right. You were very fond of that cat, weren't you?' he asked.

Pouring hot water into the three mugs, Mandy nodded. 'She *was* lovely . . . She had this funny wheezy purr – and it seemed extra loud when we made a fuss of her.' Mandy smiled as she remembered the tabby's rather eccentric habits. 'Bathsheba accompanied Reverend Madeley to every church service, you know. She always sat at the top of the steps leading down to the crypt, where she could keep an eye on everything.'

Mandy picked up her mug and clasped her hands round its warmth. 'James was very fond of Bathsheba, too,' she added. James Hunter was Mandy's best friend. He was in the year below her at Walton Moor School. 'It was James who noticed that Bathsheba looked just like the cat gargoyle.'

'Cat gargoyle?' her mum queried.

'There's one on the wall, above the crypt steps,' Mandy explained. 'It's got a round face and big eyes – just like Bathsheba.'

Mr Hope sipped his hot chocolate 'Well, then, I think the case is solved!' he concluded, giving Mandy one of his lopsided smiles. 'Take one missing cat, who had the odd habit of sitting outside a crypt, one animal-lover with a vivid imagination – and what have you got?'

Mandy blushed. 'OK. I guess you're right.' Her dad's summing-up made good sense. Bathsheba's running away *had* been preying on her mind a lot.

Mrs Hope put an arm round Mandy and gave her a cuddle. 'Drink up. Then we can all get back to bed.'

'And Bathsheba might still turn up, love,' Mr Hope added reassuringly. 'It's not that unusual for cats to go walkabout. I've known missing pets to turn up right out of the blue, weeks after they first went missing.'

'I know,' Mandy replied.' I just wish there was something more that James and I could do.'

'You two haven't exactly been idle,' Mrs Hope observed. 'Those cards you've pinned up on the school noticeboard and in Walton post office should attract attention.'

'Your mum's right, love,' said Mr Hope. 'Try not to worry about Bathsheba for the time being. OK?'

'OK,' Mandy agreed. It was good advice, as usual. Her mum and dad usually managed to put things into perspective.

A few minutes later everyone trudged back upstairs.

Mandy climbed into bed and pulled the quilt up to her chin. Mystery solved, she thought. Except for one thing. James was as worried about Bathsheba as she was. So how come *he* hadn't been having strange dreams?

Mandy and James were making their way to school the following day. It was a cold January morning. The pavements were glittery with frost and their breath made clouds in the cold air.

'Can you remember what you dreamed about last night?' Mandy thought she'd check James out. If he had seen the pale cat in his dreams, then she'd know that something very odd was going on.

'I certainly can!' James nodded, his face dead serious.

Mandy was all attention. 'What? Tell me.'

'I was at this marshmallow-eating contest,' James said in a hushed voice. 'It was terrible. I was cramming giant marshmallows into my mouth like crazy. Then I woke up and found—'

'—that you were trying to swallow your pillow!' Mandy finished. 'Ha ha. Very funny.'

'Oh, you've heard it!' James grinned at her, his eyes sparkling behind his glasses. 'Sorry. Couldn't resist that. Seriously though – did you have that spooky cat dream again?'

'Yes. And this time it woke me up,' Mandy replied. Briefly she ran through the previous night's happenings. 'But after I went back to bed I slept like a log. I think talking about it with Mum and Dad helped. They seem convinced that once I stop worrying about Bathsheba these dreams will stop.'

'It's going to be hard *not* to worry about her,' James said seriously. 'I mean – I keep thinking that she could be lying hurt somewhere.'

'Me too,' Mandy replied, shifting her schoolbag to her other shoulder. 'Or maybe she's wandered off and got lost or shut in somewhere. Starving or injured – I don't know which is worse!'

'Well, I reckon she'll try to find her way back to Walton vicarage,' James said firmly. 'Remember that story in the *Yorkshire Post* last week, about a cat who climbed into a van and got driven hundreds of miles away from its home? It found its way back to its owners again! Some scientist said cats can follow invisible magnetic lines or something.'

It was a good theory, Mandy thought, but James was forgetting something. 'Bathsheba's owner won't be waiting for her, though, James . . .'

'That's true,' James said glumly. 'Is Mrs King still keeping an eye out for her?'

Mandy had heard that Mrs King, the Walton Parish Church secretary, had been looking out for Bathsheba to take her in. 'I think so,' Mandy replied. 'But the vicarage is all locked up now.'

James frowned. 'So what would Bathsheba do if she did come back?'

Mandy thought for a while. 'I reckon she'd stay around the churchyard. It would be familiar ground for her. She used to spend lots of time in there, between services.'

'Makes sense,' James agreed. 'There would be mice to catch and somewhere to shelter.'

'But it would still be freezing in this weather.' Mandy bit her lip, then she brightened up. 'Hey, what if *we* kept a check on the churchyard? Then if Bathsheba turns up we can rescue her.'

'Good idea,' James nodded, pushing his glasses more firmly on to his nose.

'Right, then,' Mandy said, warming to the idea. 'We'll start as soon as school finishes. OK?'

'OK,' James said. 'But it'll be getting dark when we finish school. It could be pretty creepy in the churchyard.'

'You're not scared, are you?' Mandy joked.

'Who, me?' James squared his shoulders and pushed his floppy dark fringe off his face. '*As if!* See you later.'

Dusk had gathered under the winter sky when Mandy met up with James after school. They went straight along to the churchyard.

Walton Parish Church had stood for hundreds of years. It was only a couple of minutes' walk from Walton Moor School.

Mandy and James looked up at the gothic outline of its stone walls and tower, black against the darkening winter sky. The light of a nearby streetlamp hardly lit the churchyard at all.

'Just remember what Grandad says,' Mandy

said, looking at the assorted gravestones jutting out of the shadows.

'What's that?' James asked.

'The dead can't hurt anyone,' she replied, sounding calmer than she felt.

'Oh, right. That really makes me feel better,' James murmured.

'Come on,' Mandy said, gathering her courage in both hands. 'We've been in here heaps of times in the daylight. Let's go in through the lychgate.'

'Ooh-ee-ooh,' James hummed, glancing up as

they passed under the roofed main gateway into the churchyard. 'This is where the coffin and pall-bearers wait for the vicar to arrive,' he said in a hollow, spooky voice.

'I know,' Mandy said, giving him a shove. 'You can't frighten me, James Hunter!'

There was a huge yew tree in the churchyard and the spreading branches cast gloomy shadows over the rows of gravestones.

The grass crunched below their feet as they began looking around. Mandy was thinking that it would be a good idea to bring a torch next time, when suddenly a large, pale shape swooped out of the yew tree. It loomed towards them out of the darkness, silent and ghostly.

'Argh!' James gave a strangled cry and almost collided with Mandy. His fingers dug into her arm. 'What's that?'

Mandy's stomach clenched with fright. She watched the shape dip low over the graves, then it glided up to the church roof. 'Oh,' she let out a relieved sigh. 'It's only an owl, you idiot!'

'Phew!' James relaxed his grip. 'I nearly had a heart attack then! Er . . . do you think we could hurry up a bit? It's freezing and I'm starving hungry.'

'You always are!' Mandy replied. 'It'll be quicker if we split up. I'll go and look around the outside of the church. Bathsheba might be sheltering in a doorway or in one of the nooks and crannies near the bell-tower.'

'Right then. I'll check out these gravestones,' James said. 'Meet you back here in fifteen minutes? Call out if you find anything.'

'OK,' Mandy called over her shoulder as she set off down the frosty path.

The shadows were inky-black under the stone archway. As Mandy's eyes adjusted to the gloom, she could see the empty porch and the ancient door; all brass-studded oak.

'Bathsheba! Puss, puss, puss!' she called, as she searched.

There was no answering miaow, no sign of a big tabby cat. Mandy worked her way around the outside of the church, looking into each dark hollow and crevice where a cat might shelter.

James was calling out Bathsheba's name too, as he worked his way up and down the rows of headstones. His voice sounded lost and eerie in the empty churchyard.

Just then, as the moon slid behind a cloud, pitching the church and churchyard into deeper darkness, a streak of light seemed to dart past Mandy. She swallowed hard and turned her head. *What was that?*

There was nothing there now. Maybe she had imagined it. Mandy was beginning to wish she hadn't suggested that she and James split up.

She was relieved when, a few minutes later, she reached the front main gate and saw James waiting there.

'Any luck?' he asked at once. He was blowing on his fingers to warm them.

Mandy shook her head. 'I've checked everywhere. How about you?'

James shook his head.

Mandy sighed, disappointed again.

'We could call in again on our way to school tomorrow,' James suggested.

'OK,' Mandy agreed. 'I'll meet you half an hour earlier, shall I? That'll give us loads of time to have a good look.'

James nodded. 'Right. And I'll borrow one

of Dad's torches, in case we need to come back tomorrow afternoon.'

'Good idea,' Mandy said, as they began walking towards the bus stop. 'I'll bring one too. My dad's got one of those flashlight things, in case the Land-rover breaks down.'

The bus into Welford dropped them at the Fox and Goose bus stop and Mandy and James went their separate ways.

Mandy made for the narrow lane that led to Animal Ark and pulled her scarf round her chilled face. 'Wherever you are, Bathsheba,' she said under her breath, 'I hope it's somewhere warm and dry.'

Two

'Over a week of coming here, twice a day,' James said glumly, as he and Mandy began their after-school search, 'and all we've got is frostbite! No one's replied to those cards we put up at school and in the post office, either. I'm starting to think all this might be a waste of time.'

'I know what you mean,' Mandy said quietly as she peered into the gloom of the churchyard. 'Oh!' she cried, catching a sudden movement out of the corner of her eye.

She turned quickly, just in time to see a slim, pale shape slipping through the trees. 'Did you see that?' she asked James.

James looked around. 'What?'

Mandy gave a shiver. 'I thought I saw . . . something.'

'Well, there's nothing there now,' James said.

Mandy nodded. James was right. 'You know,' she said collecting herself, 'I still have this strong feeling that Bathsheba will come back. We can't give up yet.'

'I didn't mean that we should stop coming here.' James flashed her a grin. 'I was just having a moan!'

Mandy grinned back. That was one of the things she liked about James; he never stayed grumpy for long. She knew he was just as impatient as she was to find out what had happened to Bathsheba. 'Come on,' she said. 'If we've finished here we might as well go home.'

'Right . . .' Suddenly James stiffened. 'Hang about. A light's just come on in the vicarage. And did you see that?' He swung his torch over to the trees.

'What?' Mandy peered through the trees to where James was pointing. 'I can't see anything.'

'I can!' James said. 'Over there. Come on!' He sprinted away.

Mandy followed at a run. Just then, in the wavering beam of James's torch, she glimpsed something too. There were shadowy movements and rustling noises over by the hedge.

She drew level with James. 'Careful,' she whispered. 'If it's Bathsheba, we don't want to scare her.'

But it was too late for that. 'What's going on?' came a startled voice.

James swerved the beam of his torch round in surprise. There, caught in the light, was a young woman holding a toddler.

'Oh, sorry!' Mandy breathed. The little boy's wide eyes stared at them from under a mop of fair hair. 'We didn't mean to scare you!'

'I think we scared each other!' the woman said. She looked at Mandy and James, her fair brows drawing together in a frown.

Mandy suddenly realised how they must look, creeping about in the churchyard with torches. Very suspect.

'We've been searching in the churchyard for

a lost cat,' she explained hurriedly. 'Haven't we, James?'

James nodded. 'Before and after school.'

'Oh, really?' The woman's face cleared. 'We came outside to find the cat that was walking around our garden – didn't we, Daniel?' she said, smiling at her little boy. 'Perhaps it's the one you're looking for, too.'

'Was it a big tabby?' Mandy asked eagerly.

'No. It was a pale colour. More of a creamy-grey,' the woman said.

'Oh,' James said, disappointed.

'Look, why don't you come inside and have a hot drink?' the woman offered, smiling. 'It's freezing out here. You can tell me all about this cat you've lost. I'm Elizabeth Jeavons, by the way. Call me Lizzy – everyone does.'

She began to make her way back up the path towards the vicarage. 'My husband Colin is the new vicar,' she continued, as Mandy and James followed. 'You've already met Daniel, here. He's cat mad!'

Mandy smiled at the little boy. 'Hello, Daniel.'

'Pussy cat!' Daniel said promptly, his chubby cheeks dimpling in a smile.

'I'm Mandy Hope,' Mandy said, as Lizzy led the way into the vicarage kitchen. 'My mum and dad are vets in Welford village, a couple of miles down the road.'

James introduced himself. 'I live in Welford too,' he explained. 'Mandy and I go to school here in Walton.'

'Pleased to meet you both,' Lizzy smiled. 'Sounds like we're almost neighbours!' She gestured around the kitchen. 'You'll have to excuse the state of this place. We haven't finished unpacking yet and we've got decorators in. Kevin and Jim are doing a great job, but everything's going to be in a mess for weeks to come!'

Mandy saw that old Reverend Madeley's dark and rather heavy furniture had disappeared. Piles of pale wood, cupboard doors and furniture were stacked against a wall. Paint pots, brushes and piles of newspaper covered the kitchen surfaces. Boxes were heaped just anyhow. It was a mess all right, but a homely, welcome sort of a mess.

Lizzy settled Daniel in his highchair and gave him a biscuit, then she filled the kettle. 'Sit down if you can clear a space,' she said cheerfully.

Mandy and James sat on upturned wooden boxes, while Lizzy made some tea. Daniel sucked the end of his biscuit, then held out the soggy mess to James.

'Er . . . No thanks,' James said, going a bit pink.

Mandy tried to keep a straight face. James could cope with anything to do with animals. He'd seen animals being born, and watched her dad sew up no end of gory wounds, but lively toddlers threw him into a panic.

Lizzy poured tea into two mugs and set them on a tray with a plate of biscuits. 'I'll just pop these into the sitting-room. I expect Kevin and Jim are ready for a cuppa.'

She reappeared a few moments later and took some cake out of one of the boxes. 'Help yourselves,' she smiled. 'It's not as nice as home-made, but I haven't time even to think about baking at the moment!'

After pouring more tea, Lizzy sat down on another box. 'So who does the cat you're looking for belong to?' she asked.

Mandy helped herself to a slice of cake. 'Reverend Madeley,' she explained. 'Bathsheba's the big tabby who used to live here at the vicarage. Everyone in Walton knew her. She used to go to all the church services.'

'Ah, yes,' Lizzy said, thoughtfully. 'Someone mentioned that Reverend Madeley used to have a cat. Sounds like she was quite a character.'

'Oh, she was,' James said, munching his cake. 'She used to sit at the top of the steps leading down to the crypt during each service. Reverend Madeley used to say she was keeping an eye on everyone,' James smiled. 'But no one's seen her since the Reverend died. She just upped and left.'

'Yes, but now, if she does come back, she'll find someone to feed and care for her,' Mandy said delightedly. 'So she might decide to stay.'

Looking uncomfortable, Lizzy poured some milk into a cup and gave it to Daniel. 'I'll certainly keep my eye open for a big tabby cat,' she said. 'But I'm afraid I can't promise anything else . . .'

Mandy stared at her. Did that mean that Bathsheba was no longer welcome at the vicarage? She threw a questioning glance at James.

He shrugged his shoulders in a 'search-me' gesture.

'You don't happen to know who owns that creamy-grey cat that Daniel and I saw earlier, do you?' Lizzy asked, clearly changing the subject. 'We heard it calling out, but the moment it saw us, it high-tailed into the churchyard. We were out looking for it when you almost bumped into us.'

'Pussy cat!' Daniel said chirpily, beaming from under a milky moustache. 'Pussy cat!'

Lizzy chuckled. 'Listen to him! Like I said, he's cat mad.'

Mandy saw an opportunity. 'Daniel would *love* Bathsheba, then!' she said straight away. 'She has this funny-sounding miaow. It's all sort of creaky and wheezy. And she's really friendly with everybody . . .'

Lizzy looked even more uncomfortable. 'Oh dear. I know what you're getting at, Mandy. I'd love to help, but I think I'd better explain before you go any further. Cats are a bit of a sore point around here. We've talked about getting one.

I'm as fond of them as Daniel is, but Colin's really not keen on the idea. He's allergic to a lot of them, you see.'

Mandy and James exchanged dismayed glances. So if Bathsheba ever *did* come back, she was going to find herself without a home!

'I'm sorry,' Lizzy said, sounding genuinely apologetic. 'But that's how things stand. I'm afraid Colin was rather relieved to hear that Reverend Madeley's old cat had taken itself off somewhere.'

I bet he was, Mandy thought, raising her eyebrows at James. *That meant he didn't have to bother about getting rid of her!*

As Lizzy went to fetch another biscuit for Daniel, a man with a thin face and untidy brown hair came into the kitchen, carrying a tray with two empty mugs. He was wearing glasses and paint-splattered overalls.

'Thanks very much for the tea, Mrs Jeavons,' he said, with a friendly smile for Mandy and James. 'Hi, there.'

'Hi,' they replied.

'Ah, Kevin. You haven't met Mandy and James. They've just been telling me about a lost cat they've been searching for. A large female tabby, called Bathsheba. I thought maybe you and Jim wouldn't mind keeping an eye open for her.'

'We think she might come back to the churchyard,' Mandy explained.

'She used to live at the vicarage,' James added.

'Sure, we'll keep a lookout. No problem,' Kevin said. 'Me and Jim are in and out all day with materials and what not. If we see a tabby, you'll be the first to know. Leave a telephone number with Mrs Jeavons, if you like.'

'We will. Thanks very much,' Mandy said.

'No problem,' Kevin said again. It seemed to be his favourite phrase. 'I know what it's like to lose a pet. I'm a real animal-lover, me. Got a fair few of my own.'

'Have you?' Mandy said, immediately interested. 'What have you got?'

'Have you got an hour to spare?' Kevin said. 'No, seriously – I've got three cats, two dogs, a garter snake, a rabbit, ten terrapins, a chameleon, and a cockatiel at the moment!'

'Cripes!' James said. 'I have enough trouble looking after my cat and dog.'

'Are you running an animal sanctuary?' Mandy asked.

'Nah! Sometimes it feels like it though!' Kevin chuckled. 'My wife, Amy, reckons we'll have to move to a larger house if I get any more pets. Trouble is, people know I love animals. They bring me any they don't want. And you can't refuse, can you? Amy reckons I'm a proper soft touch, but I don't care.' Looking at his paint-splattered watch, he made for the door. 'Anyway, must get back to work. Nice to meet you two.'

'And you,' Mandy and James replied.

The decorator went back out into the hall. They could hear him whistling.

'Kevin seems to live for those animals of his,' Lizzy said. 'Especially his dogs. He says they go everywhere with him. He even brings them to work with him.'

Mandy raised her eyebrows. She imagined two dogs curled up in the sitting-room, watching patiently while Kevin shinned up and down a ladder with paint and brushes. 'Don't you mind?' she asked.

'How do you mean? Oh, I see!' Lizzy

chuckled. 'He doesn't bring them in the house. They stay outside in his van,' she explained.

Mandy had noticed a large white van parked just outside the vicarage, but she hadn't taken much notice of it. *That's awful!* she thought, beginning to revise her opinion of Kevin. 'All day? They must get really bored.'

Lizzy shook her head. 'Don't worry,' she smiled. 'Kevin takes really good care of those dogs. They're real characters – just like him.'

Mandy glanced at James. It couldn't be right, keeping two dogs in a van all day and in this freezing cold weather. She decided they had to check this out. From the look on James's face, she saw that he was thinking the same thing.

'Would you like more tea?' Lizzy asked.

'No thank you,' they answered politely.

Mandy was ready to jump up and dash straight outside, but she pushed herself slowly to her feet. 'We ought to go now or we'll be late for supper, won't we, James?'

James nodded quickly.

'If you hang on a minute, Colin will be back,' Lizzy said. 'He'd love to meet you both. And

I'm sure he wouldn't mind running you home in the car.'

'Thanks,' James said. 'But we don't mind catching the bus. We're used to it.'

Lizzy saw them to the door. 'I expect you'll meet Colin soon anyway. He's doing a guest assembly at Walton Moor School tomorrow morning.'

'I can't wait,' Mandy whispered, so that only James could hear.

'Er . . . Right then, we'll be off,' James said hastily. 'Thanks for the tea and cake.'

'Yes, thanks. The cake was lovely,' Mandy said, remembering her manners.

At the doorway, Lizzy waved goodbye with Daniel in her arms. The little boy waved a pudgy hand as they opened the front gate. 'Bye! Bye!' he shouted.

Mandy and James waved back. 'Bye, Daniel!'

'Come and see us again,' Lizzy called. 'We love to have visitors.'

Mandy and James waited until Lizzy had gone back into the vicarage then hurried towards the decorators' van.

Mandy shaded her eyes as she peered into

the back window. It was dark inside, but she could see the shapes of a ladder and other equipment. 'I can't see any dogs,' she said.

James was round at the side of the van. 'Me neither. This window's all misted up.'

'Hey! What's your game!' a loud voice called out.

Mandy and James nearly jumped out of their skins. They saw Kevin running towards them, a plastic carrier bag swinging from his hand.

'Oh, it's you two,' he said. 'Sorry. I thought it was kids mucking about with the van. You can't be too careful. There's valuable equipment in here.' He unlocked the back doors, saying, 'I expect you're wanting to meet Becky and Ben. Did Mrs Jeavons tell you about them?'

Mandy nodded, still feeling anxious. How on earth could two dogs fit inside this loaded van? She steeled herself for whatever was to come . . .

'Here you go!' Kevin said, as the doors swung open. 'Meet my two Yorkies. Becky and Ben – short for Rebecca and Benjamin.'

Mandy's eyes opened wide. Nestled in a corner of the van was a dog basket, lined with fleecy fabric. Two small, sleepy heads poked out from beneath a layer of blankets. 'Oh, they're gorgeous,' she breathed, looking at the tiny faces. Enormous dark eyes peeped out of tousled chestnut fur.

Mandy had been imagining a couple of collies or spaniels, not miniature Yorkshire terriers.

'Time for another walk, guys,' Kevin said.

At the word 'walk' the dogs jumped out from beneath the blankets, shook themselves and trotted happily over to their master, wagging their tails. Kevin took two little plaid coats from beside the basket and slipped them on to the dogs, then clipped on their leads.

Mandy was wondering what Kevin had in his plastic carrier. But she didn't have to wait long to find out.

Kevin took out an old-fashioned pottery hot-water bottle. He tucked it beneath the dogs' blankets. 'Holds the heat better than those modern rubber things,' he explained. 'Becky and Ben like to come back to a nice warm bed, don't you? And in this weather I keep a water bottle tucked in next to them all the time.'

The Yorkies yapped and jumped up at Kevin, whom they obviously adored.

'Can we stroke them?' Mandy asked.

'Sure, no problem,' Kevin said. 'Soft as butter, these two are. They've been coming to work with me ever since they were pups. Now they're getting on a bit, you'd think they'd rather stay at home in front of the fire, wouldn't you? But no. I tried that and they just cried all day. So Amy says, "You'd better take them with you." '

Kevin grinned. 'I don't mind really. I pop outside, now and then, to make sure they're warm enough and take them for a couple of walks. And they're happy as anything.'

As she and James stroked the dogs, Mandy had to admit that Becky and Ben looked content and well cared for.

'Right, off we go, guys,' Kevin said to the Yorkies. 'Bye now, you two. See you later.'

'Bye!' Mandy and James gave each of the dogs a final pat. They watched him walk the tiny dogs down the street.

'That's a relief,' James breathed. 'For a minute back there, I thought you were about to give him a lecture about cruelty to dogs!'

'I would have,' Mandy said. 'But he didn't need it!'

'You know, Kevin reminds me of someone,' James said, as they headed towards the bus stop. He had a gleam in his eye. 'Can't think who. Someone else who's completely animal mad . . .'

'Does their name begin with "M" by any chance?' Mandy said.

'Now that you mention it . . .' James was grinning from ear to ear.

Mandy gave him a playful shove.

'Just kidding,' James said, rubbing his arm. 'Kevin's great, isn't he? And Lizzy and Daniel are really nice too.'

'Yes,' Mandy agreed. 'But I'm not looking forward to meeting the new vicar. It's a shame he's not more like Kevin. Then Bathsheba would still have a home to go to.'

Three

'So what's the verdict?' Mr Hope asked that evening, as he mixed milk and butter into a pan of mashed potatoes. 'Is Walton's new vicar trendy or traditional? Backward-looking or forward-thinking?'

Mandy had just finished telling him about meeting Lizzy and Daniel in the churchyard. She was setting out plates and cutlery. It was her mum's turn to do the late surgery, so her dad was making supper.

'I don't know.' She shrugged. 'James and I left before Reverend Jeavons came home.'

Mr Hope gave her a questioning look. 'Why do I get the feeling that you're not too keen on him?'

'Who, *me*?' Mandy said.

'Yes, *you*,' Mr Hope replied. 'I know that expression. Come on. Out with it.'

'Well – he's probably all right . . .' Mandy said, putting salt and pepper on the table, '. . . if you don't mind cat-haters.'

'Aha,' Mr Hope said, his dark eyes twinkling. 'So that's it. The poor man's already on your blacklist and you haven't even met him. Doesn't sound very fair to me.'

Mandy coloured. Her dad had a way of choosing just the right words to make her examine her conscience. It was really annoying at times. 'Reverend Jeavons is glad Bathsheba's gone missing,' she said indignantly. 'I don't call that fair, either!'

Mr Hope opened the oven door and lifted out a cheese and mushroom pie. 'Smells good enough to eat,' he announced. 'I expect there's a reason for the new vicar's aversion to cats.'

'Well – Lizzy did say that Reverend Jeavons is allergic to some of them,' Mandy murmured.

'Hmm. Allergies can be pretty nasty, you know.' Mr Hope finished mashing the potatoes and began to drain a saucepan of green beans. 'Coughing and sneezing's not the half of it. With a bad allergic reaction the nose and throat tissues can swell. It's very uncomfortable and sometimes makes breathing difficult.'

'Really? I suppose it would be pretty awful if being around cats made you feel that bad,' Mandy admitted. If it wasn't for Bathsheba, she thought, she could almost feel sorry for the new vicar. 'I'm just glad I'm not allergic to any animals.'

Mr Hope began dishing out the food. 'Me too,' he said with a grin. 'Otherwise I'd be looking for someone to take over Animal Ark!'

Mandy gave her dad a mock fierce look. 'Don't even think about it!'

Emily Hope came in from the surgery. She took off her lab coat and hung it behind the door. 'Hi, you two. Any luck with finding Bathsheba, Mandy?'

Mandy shook her head. Over supper, she told her mum and dad about meeting Kevin, and

Becky and Ben, his miniature Yorkies.

'He must be devoted to them, to go to so much trouble,' Mrs Hope commented.

After clearing away the supper things, Mandy went into the sitting-room and curled up with a wildlife magazine. She loved this room. There was a roaring fire in the big stone inglenook fireplace and red-patterned carpets on the stone floor made the place really cosy.

'I hate to mention it, but haven't you got any homework to do?' Mr Hope asked an hour later.

Mandy pulled a face. 'Just a bit of maths.'

'Hadn't you better go upstairs and do it then?' her dad prompted.

Mandy groaned, but she jumped up and grabbed her schoolbag. James was brilliant at maths, but she really had to work at it!

The following morning, Mandy filed into the school hall with her classmates.

She saw James sitting in the row in front, over by a window, and waved. He waved back, then pulled a face and pointed to the front of the hall.

Mandy turned her head and saw that the headteacher, Mr Wakeham, was walking on to the stage. He looked a little annoyed.

'Good morning,' Mr Wakeham began. 'We were to have a special guest assembly this morning, but I'm afraid he hasn't arrived yet . . .' He paused as there was a slight commotion to one side of the stage.

Mandy saw that another teacher was hurriedly ushering a large, broad-shouldered man on to the stage. He had sandy hair and was wearing jeans and a sweatshirt. His friendly gaze swept over the crowded hall as he walked over to greet a surprised-looking Mr Wakeham.

A few seconds later, the Head made an announcement. 'Well it seems that Reverend Jeavons *will* be taking assembly. But first, let's give him a warm welcome.'

'He looks nice, doesn't he?' she heard someone behind her say.

Mandy didn't want to admit it, but he did. She was caught off-guard. She had been ready to dislike Reverend Jeavons on sight from what she'd heard about him. She'd expected him to be thin and stooped and miserable-looking – and probably wear a stuffy suit. But if anything, he reminded her of her own easy-going father.

As Mr Wakeham went to sit at the side of the stage, Reverend Jeavons smiled out at his audience. 'Good morning, everyone,' he began. 'I'm Colin Jeavons, the new vicar at Walton Parish Church. Sorry I'm a little late, but my son Daniel trod in some paint and I had to help clear up before it dried . . .' He rolled his eyes, then smiled.

There was a ripple of laughter. Mandy noticed that Mr Wakeham didn't join in. In fact, thought Mandy, the sight of the new vicar wearing jeans seemed to have thrown the head into a state of shock!

'I'm looking forward to getting to know you all,' Reverend Jeavons continued. 'And once the vicarage emerges from under a sea of paint and dustsheets, I hope some of you will come and visit me and my family . . .'

Mandy found herself enjoying morning assembly more than she usually did. Reverend Jeavons had chosen the theme of the lost sheep.

Somehow, his version of the story was really interesting. It even made her laugh! Time seemed to fly by.

When assembly was over, the head thanked Reverend Jeavons and then everyone filed out and went back to their form rooms.

'Did you see Mr Wakeham's face when he realised the guy in the jeans and sweatshirt was Walton's new vicar?' giggled one of Mandy's classmates.

Mandy nodded, smiling herself. 'It did seem strange, at first. But I like it.'

'Yeah! Me too,' came the reply. 'Makes the vicar seem almost human.'

Mandy laughed.

'Assembly was much better than normal,' said another. 'Usually it's just boring old stories we've heard before.'

As Mandy sorted out her books for the first lesson, she had mixed feelings about Reverend Jeavons. He had certainly been a big hit with everyone in her class. She wondered what James had made of him.

'The new vicar seemed OK,' James said, as they

walked towards the churchyard after school. 'I mean, he's not a monster or anything.'

'No, I suppose not.' Mandy was still not quite ready to admit that she had liked Reverend Jeavons.

Pausing at the covered main gate, Mandy took her dad's flashlight out of her schoolbag. It wasn't quite dark, but there were deep shadows between the graves and in the arches and hollows over by the church itself.

'Hello there, you two!' a voice called out. 'I thought you might call by.'

Mandy and James saw a large figure, holding a much smaller one by the hand. It was Reverend Jeavons and Daniel.

'It looks like he's been waiting for us,' James said, looking a bit worried.

'Maybe he doesn't think we should be hanging around the churchyard,' Mandy said.

The vicar and his son reached them, their breath steaming in the cold air. 'You must be Mandy and James,' Reverend Jeavons said. 'Lizzy told me all about meeting you here yesterday. She says you've been coming here for two weeks or so.'

Mandy nodded. 'That's right. We've been looking for Bathsheba.'

'Do you really think that cat will come back here now?' the vicar asked. 'Isn't it more likely that she's found herself a new family?'

Mandy shook her head. 'Not Bathsheba,' she said firmly. 'This is where she belongs. Isn't it, James?'

James nodded and settled his glasses more firmly on to his nose.

The vicar looked down at them, a slight frown drawing his sandy brows together. 'You two seem very sure about that.'

'We are,' Mandy said promptly.

'In that case, could you use some help? I've an hour free. Daniel and I were just going for a walk.' He smiled. 'To be truthful, it's nice to be away from paint fumes and sawdust. It's like a demolition site in our kitchen!'

Mandy and James laughed, then nodded.

'Has anyone thought to check inside the church too?' the vicar asked. 'There have been lots of comings and goings around here lately, as we've been settling in – and I, for one, don't always shut the door behind me.'

'I hadn't thought of that,' Mandy said. Mrs King, the church secretary, would have checked inside the church when Bathsheba first went missing. Then, during the weeks until Reverend Jeavons had arrived, the church had been kept locked. 'No, not recently,' she added. But the vicar was right. With all the recent comings and goings, Bathsheba could have slipped in without anyone seeing her.

'OK,' Reverend Jeavons said. 'We'll check inside too.'

Mandy looked at James. 'OK,' she said. 'That would be great.'

'Yes.' James blinked. 'Thanks, Vicar.'

'Oh, call me Colin,' the vicar said, with a grin. 'All my friends do. Right. Where shall we start?'

'Well – usually, one of us checks round the graves and the other looks round the outside of the church,' Mandy explained.

Colin nodded. 'How about if Daniel and I check the outside of the church?' he suggested. 'We could meet you by the front door when you've finished checking the churchyard. Then we'll go inside together.'

'Fine by us,' Mandy and James replied.

Colin swept Daniel up in his arms, then strode off towards the church; a large, bulky figure in his thick coat. They could hear the two of them laughing. Then Daniel's high-pitched voice rang out in answer to something his father said.

Mandy and James did their usual search. It didn't take long. They knew the churchyard by heart now; every gravestone, every crack in every stone plinth. They checked under hedges and in the hollows of the yew tree's exposed roots.

At one point, Mandy caught sight of a sleek, pale-grey shape just as it disappeared under a hedge. She thought it might be the cat that Lizzy and Daniel had seen yesterday. But there was no sign of Bathsheba.

'Brrr,' James shivered. 'Let's go and find Colin.'

'OK.' Mandy was just as eager to get out of the freezing churchyard.

'Find anything?' Colin said as he unlocked the church door.

Mandy shook her head.

'But you're not about to give up?' Colin guessed, his footsteps echoing on the marble floor as he walked down the nave. 'I admire your staying power.'

The new vicar might not be keen on cats, Mandy thought, but he was going to an awful lot of trouble to help them look for Bathsheba.

Ten minutes later, they had searched everywhere; the gaps between the pews, the choir stalls, the little side chapel.

Colin and Daniel emerged from a room to

one side of the altar. 'No sign of any cat in there,' Colin reported. 'But I think we ought to check the crypt before we call it a day. The wrought-iron entrance gate is always kept closed – but I imagine that a cat might be able to slip right through it. The spaces between the wrought-iron pattern are a few inches wide in parts.'

Mandy and James looked at each other. They hadn't thought of that either.

'This is where Bathsheba liked to sit,' Mandy said, as they reached the top of the steps leading down to the crypt.

'She must be a very special cat, for you to care about her so much,' Colin said.

'She is,' Mandy replied. 'She came to all the services. Coming here just won't be the same without her.'

Colin nodded. 'I can imagine that. But I'd really appreciate it if you'd both come along here on Sunday morning.'

Mandy and James looked at him questioningly.

'Reverend Hadcroft has kindly offered to bring his Welford congregation over here to

Walton on Sunday morning – to support my
first service here,' Colin explained. 'He's really
doing his best to make me welcome. The church
should be packed with parishioners from
Walton *and* Welford. I'm a bit nervous actually,'
he confided. 'Seeing a couple more friendly
faces in the congregation will help to settle my
butterflies!'

Mandy and James smiled. 'We'll be here,' they
promised.

'You will?' Colin beamed all over his face.
'Jolly good! I know Lizzy and Daniel will be
pleased to see you again. Right then . . .' He
switched on the light at the top of the crypt
steps. The steps and crypt entrance were
suddenly bathed in a gentle light. 'I'll go down
first, and open the gate,' he said. 'Could you
bring Daniel for me?'

Mandy and James nodded, each taking one
of the toddler's hands.

'Daddy won't be long,' Mandy said to the
toddler, who smiled cheekily up at her,
then watched his father as he went down the
stairs.

'Wow! I never realised it was all fancy like

that,' James said, as Colin opened the wrought-iron entrance gate to the crypt.

Mandy looked down and saw that the entrance *was* very grand. Two stone angels stood guard, one either side of an archway wreathed in delicately carved ivy. 'Me neither,' she replied. 'You can't see it properly without the light on.'

They made their way slowly down the steps, at Daniel's pace.

'Goodness! It's chilly down here!' Colin's voice from inside the crypt came echoing hollowly up the stairs.

'Er . . . It sounds a bit creepy down there, too!' James whispered. 'Are we sure we want to do this?'

Mandy gave him a fierce look. It did sound creepy, but if there was a possibility that Bathsheba could be down there, someone should go and see.

Recognising the look, James squared his shoulders. 'OK. Let's go, then.'

Despite the brightly lit entrance, it was gloomy in the body of the crypt. Mandy smelled dusty old stone and another smell, like dry leaves. A chill crept down her back.

'Cripes!' James said in a wobbly voice. 'It's like a cave down here.'

It was true, Mandy thought, looking around. It was much bigger than she had expected.

The floor was made of huge stone slabs and the vaulted ceiling soared overhead. There were rows of stone tombs, topped with ancient carvings of long-dead noblemen and women. More caskets were stacked in shadowy niches set into the stone walls.

'There must be heaps of places a cat could hide down here,' Mandy said with dismay.

'Cat!' Daniel repeated, recognising the word.

'Don't worry, we'll help you look,' Colin said cheerfully, as he swung the toddler back into his arms. 'Oh, you might need those torches in some of these dark corners. And watch out for cobwebs!'

'I bet there are some juicy spiders down here. We should have brought them a few flies!' James tried to calm his nerves with one of his terrible jokes.

'Ha-ha!' Mandy swallowed hard. She didn't mind spiders in the garden in daylight. But the thought of them dangling from huge webs that were waiting to brush against her face or tangle in her hair was another thing entirely.

'Are you all right, Mandy?' Colin asked. 'You look a bit anxious.'

'No, I'm fine,' Mandy said sharply. 'Well, no . . . it is a bit creepy,' she admitted, smiling sheepishly.

'But it's . . . um . . . interesting,' James added, trying to put on a brave face.

Colin chuckled. 'Can these be the same two intrepid characters who've been searching round a dark and gloomy graveyard for the past two weeks? I should think that took some courage!'

Mandy and James grinned. Put like that, the crypt didn't seem so spooky. Daniel certainly didn't mind it. He was hanging on to his dad's shoulder and looking around with interest.

They spent the next few minutes peering into alcoves and looking behind stone tombs. They disturbed layers of powdery, ancient dust and even saw a centipede scurrying away to find cover. But there was no sign of a cat.

'Bathsheba! Puss, puss!' Mandy called out. But no distinctive wheezy miaow answered her.

'I don't think she's down here,' Colin said eventually, when they'd looked everywhere. 'Sorry, guys.'

He sounded genuinely disappointed. Mandy couldn't help it. 'But, I thought you hated cats!' she blurted out. The thought had been on her mind since Colin first met them in the churchyard and offered to join in the search.

Colin didn't seem to mind. 'I'm afraid it's more that they don't agree with me,' he replied. 'I only have to be in the same room with one and I start coughing and sneezing like an old steam engine! My doctor says I'm probably not allergic to all cats. But I've yet to meet one whose company I can bear for more than a few minutes!'

'What a shame,' Mandy said. 'Lizzy told us that she and Daniel love cats.'

'That's true.' Colin nodded 'They'd love one, Daniel especially. But it's just not on, I'm afraid.' Mandy could see the regret in his eyes.

'Anyway,' Colin said, cheering up. 'Daniel's quite happy at the moment just to wave at cats that come into the garden – like the creamy-grey one.'

'Oh,' Mandy said. 'Has that cat been back again? I wonder who it belongs to.'

'No idea,' Colin said. 'Lizzy puts food out for it, but it never eats anything. So it's unlikely to be a stray. It must be getting fed elsewhere. But it seems to be really shy. Every time Lizzy takes Daniel outside to make a fuss of it, it disappears.'

James hadn't been listening. He was bending over a particularly impressive tomb. 'Hey! Just look at this one!' he said eagerly. 'It must be ancient.'

Mandy went over to look. The carved stone figure on top of the tomb wore a headdress that framed her cheeks and covered her chin. Her hands, which rested on the rich folds of her gown, were pressed together in an attitude of prayer. 'Gosh! She's wearing a wimple,' Mandy said. 'I remember drawing one of those when we did medieval costume last year.'

'That's right,' Colin said. 'Some of these

tombs are very old indeed. This one over here is the first vicar of Walton. He went on to become quite a bigwig in the Church. When he died he wanted to come back to Walton to rest.'

Mandy and James went over to look at the vicar's tomb. On top of the tomb lay a stone, stern-faced figure, dressed in a hooded robe.

'Doesn't look like he was a bundle of fun!' James whispered, just loud enough for Mandy to hear. 'I bet he could chop wood with that face, it's so sharp-looking!'

'Don't!' Mandy almost spluttered with laughter.

'These tombs and carvings are really interesting, though,' James went on, more loudly. 'It would be great to draw them. Hey! I've just had a great idea.'

'Hmm. Sounds like this could spell trouble!' Colin said, with a twinkle in his eye.

James grinned. 'My class is doing a photography project in art,' he began. 'We each have to choose a different theme. And I was wondering . . .'

'If you could take photographs down here?'

Colin anticipated. 'I don't see why not. You can take some in the church too, if you like.'

'Really? Oh, thanks!' James said. 'Just wait until I tell the others!'

A few minutes later, they all trooped back upstairs. Mandy paused on the top step and pointed upwards. 'We call that Bathsheba's gargoyle,' she told Colin.

Colin craned his neck to look at the stone carving. 'Oh, yes. It's rather handsome, isn't it? So it must look like Bathsheba?'

James nodded.

Mandy looked at the carving more closely. It seemed to her that the stone face looked sad. It was almost as if, somehow, the gargoyle was also missing Bathsheba.

Four

The following day, Mandy was making her way to the playground to meet James at morning break when she overheard one of her classmates talking.

'Yeah, it darted right out in front of me as I was passing Walton Church – then just stood there, looking at me!'

'Excuse me for butting in,' Mandy said. 'But you weren't talking about a cat, were you?'

Sarah, the girl who had spoken, nodded. 'Mmm. Gave me the scare of my life!' she said dramatically.

'Was it Bathsheba from Walton Church?' Mandy asked excitedly.

Sarah shook her head. 'No, I've never seen it before – it was a strange creamy-grey colour and it had weird, piercing blue eyes.' She shivered.

Mandy's heart sank in disappointment that it hadn't been Bathsheba. 'What did you do?' she asked Sarah.

'I bent down to stroke it, but it kept backing away and wouldn't let me get anywhere near,' Sarah replied. 'It was a bit scary, the way it kept looking right at me – like it was studying me or something. Then it turned away suddenly and vanished back into the churchyard. It's funny, but I felt like it was dismissing me. Like – I wasn't the one it was looking for. Weird, wasn't it?'

Mandy agreed that it was.

In the playground, she told James about Sarah's experience.

'Sounds like the same cat Lizzy and Daniel keep seeing,' James commented. 'I wonder where it lives?'

Mandy shrugged. 'Somewhere near Walton Church, I'd imagine.'

'Did Sarah see where it went?' James asked.

'She said it just darted away into the churchyard,' Mandy replied.

The bell rang for the end of break. 'I'll be half an hour late leaving this afternoon,' James said. 'There's a special computer club meeting. Do you want to give the churchyard search a miss?'

'No, I'll wait for you,' Mandy replied. 'I'll call Mum and Dad to say I'll be a bit late.'

She didn't want to miss looking for Bathsheba, but neither did she fancy looking around the churchyard by herself!

Mandy was still thinking about the strange pale cat that had been seen around Walton churchyard when the bell rang for home-time.

She went to meet James in the IT room.

'Hello, Mandy,' said Mrs Ward, the teacher who ran computer club. 'This is a surprise. I didn't think you were all that interested in computers.'

Mandy smiled sheepishly. 'I've come to wait for James, actually.'

James looked up from his computer and

waved her over, but she smiled and shook her head.

'I'll be fine here,' she said, sitting down at the back of the room. 'I've got an animal magazine I can read.'

By the time computer club had finished, Mandy had read her magazine twice. She yawned and stretched as everyone filed past and out of the classroom.

Mrs Ward walked over with James. 'I've just had a thought,' she said. 'Wasn't it you two who put that card about a missing cat on the noticeboard?' she asked.

'Yes,' Mandy confirmed. 'Can you help?'

'I don't know . . .' Mrs Ward replied thoughtfully. 'It's just that I had a rather curious experience when passing the churchyard in my car this morning: a cat ran straight out into my path.' The teacher shook her head. 'Good job I was going slowly and was able to stop!' She paused for a moment. 'But it was the strangest creature . . . never seen a cat quite like it before. A creamy-grey, sort of stony colour, with the most amazing eyes – bright blue. It just stood there in the middle of the road, looking at me, then darted away. Seemed to just melt into the churchyard wall . . .'

Mandy and James looked at each other.

'Thanks very much for telling us,' Mandy said. 'But the cat we're looking for is a big tabby.'

'Oh, well. Sorry I couldn't help.' Mrs Ward smiled.

Outside school, Mandy fell in step with James and they began walking towards the churchyard.

'*Another* sighting of this strange cat,' James said. He shook his head in puzzlement. 'I wonder why *we* haven't seen it? I mean – we must have been in that churchyard heaps of times now. We practically live there!'

Suddenly, Mandy remembered the time she herself had seen a pale shape streaking through the trees. 'You know – I reckon I might have seen it, after all,' she said, thoughtfully. 'But where on earth has it come from? And why does it keep going up to people, then running away?'

James shoved his glasses on to the bridge of his nose. 'Search me,' he said. 'It can't be because it's looking for food – otherwise it would eat the food Lizzy Jeavons puts out for it.'

They walked on in silence. The cold snap still had Walton in its grip. There were icicles hanging from the drainpipes of buildings they passed. Overhead, the late afternoon sky was a sullen, leaden grey, and the light was fading fast.

The decorators' van was parked outside the vicarage. They saw that the back was open and a grey-haired man was lifting out a sack of plaster.

'That must be Jim,' Mandy said.

Jim nodded as they passed. 'How do, there.'

'Hi,' Mandy and James replied, glancing into the van for a glimpse of Becky and Ben.

Jim chuckled. 'I know what you're after. Well, they're not in there. Kevin's taken them out for their regular constitutional.'

'What's a consti . . .?' Mandy looked sideways at James.

'I think he means a walk,' James said.

'That's what I said, diddle I?' Jim went back towards the vicarage, chuckling to himself.

'Was that a joke?' James looked baffled.

Mandy grinned. 'I think so!'

The grey-haired man had just disappeared inside when they heard an unearthly yowl. Then came the sound of high-pitched yapping and growling.

'That could be Becky and Ben!' James said.

'It's coming from round the corner,' Mandy said. 'Come on, let's go and see what's happening.'

They dashed along the street and turned the corner. The churchyard wall stretched a few metres along the side street, until it gave way to some private houses.

Kevin was kneeling down on the pavement in front of the wall, trying to calm the two Yorkies.

Yap! Yap! Grr! Becky and Ben leaped about, straining against their leads. They were both out of breath, their pink tongues showing as they panted.

'Easy now, you guys,' Kevin was saying. He looked pale and shaken himself. 'It's gone now.'

Mandy and James raced up to them.

'What's wrong?' Mandy said at once.

Kevin stood up slowly, looking shaken. Becky and Ben were clutched to his chest. 'It was that weird creamy-grey cat that's been hanging around the churchyard,' he explained. 'Lizzy told me about it. Said it was very shy. So when it came running along the churchyard wall towards me, just now, I thought I'd try and give it a bit of fuss.'

He swallowed hard. 'At first, Becky and Ben sat there good as gold, as usual. They never bark at cats. They've grown up used to all kinds of animals in our house. But that weird cat rubbed them up the wrong way. I don't know if it was the bright blue eyes that spooked them, but they certainly spooked me! Seemed to go right through me!'

Mandy could see that the little Yorkies were still trembling. 'I wonder what upset them so much?'

Kevin shrugged his shoulders. 'Search me,' he replied.

'What happened to the cat?' James asked.

'I didn't really notice,' Kevin said. 'I was too busy trying to calm these guys down. It just seemed to disappear.'

'Just like with Sarah and Mrs Ward!' James said.

'Who are Sarah and Mrs Ward?' Kevin blinked from behind his glasses.

'Sarah's a schoolfriend,' Mandy explained. 'And Mrs Ward is a teacher. They both saw the cat this morning.'

Kevin rubbed his chin. 'Bit of a mystery, isn't it?'

'Maybe we'll see it this time,' James said. 'We're just about to go on our search for Bathsheba,' he explained to Kevin.

'Best of luck then,' Kevin said. 'I'd better get back to work, or Jim'll have my guts for garters. Come on, guys.'

He put the dogs down on the ground, then moved away, the dogs trotting obediently at his heels.

'See you,' Mandy and James called.

'Kevin must have been upset,' Mandy said. 'He didn't say "no problem" once.'

'It's dead weird, isn't it?' James said as they retraced their steps. 'Somehow we've ended up looking for *two* cats!'

They went through the lychgate and Mandy took a deep breath. The churchyard looked somehow unfamiliar today. They were later than usual, and in just the few minutes since they had been speaking to Kevin it had grown dark.

Overhead, the sky was almost black. The gravestones could only just be seen above a veil of mist hovering over the frozen ground.

Mandy fished her dad's flashlight out of her schoolbag. 'This is like one of those old horror films,' she said, shivering. The grey-white swirls of mist seemed to absorb the torchlight.

James clicked his torch on, too, and shone it on to the path that led between the gravestones. 'Yeah!' he agreed with a chuckle. 'Better watch out for ghosts, werewolves and vampires!'

Mandy giggled. 'Sure!'

Suddenly a haunting wail rose into the air, coming from the direction of the church. The smile froze on James's face. 'What's that?'

Her thoughts still full of werewolves and vampires, Mandy pointed her flashlight towards the church with shaking hands. She half-expected a ghoulish creature to loom out at her.

'Further over!' James gave a piercing whisper and pointed. 'Look!'

Mandy moved her beam of light a little to the left to meet James's, then gasped. A creamy-grey smoky substance was oozing out from between the stone wall of the church and the

ground. As they stared, it became a cloud that seemed to hover just above the grass. Then suddenly, the mist cleared around it, and the stone-coloured cat they'd heard so much about was standing there, large as life.

Mandy felt a shock of realisation go right through her as she met its bright blue stare. 'Oh!' she cried.

'What?' James whispered.

Mandy took a deep, shaky breath. 'I know this is going to sound unbelievable, but . . . that's the cat I've been dreaming about!'

'Cripes! Are you sure?' James looked as if he couldn't take in what Mandy had just told him.

Mandy nodded. 'Its face is always shadowed in my dreams,' she explained. 'So I hadn't noticed it has the same bright blue eyes people have been describing – but I just *know* it's the same cat.'

As if it could understand what Mandy was saying, the cat opened its mouth and let out another plaintive cry.

Mandy nodded. 'And that eerie call it has – it's the same. I should have recognised it . . .'

As if satisfied, the cat slowly turned and began to walk away gracefully.

Mandy felt rooted to the spot.

'Come on, before we lose it!' James cried in a shaky voice.

'No, wait!' Mandy hissed. 'We'll frighten it!' But it was too late. James was dashing across the churchyard in hot pursuit.

The startled cat became just a pale streak. As James's wavering torchlight fell upon the cat, Mandy could barely see it; it was the exact same colour as the stone church itself.

'Ow!' James cried suddenly, missing his step

on the damp grass. He dropped his torch and bent to pick it up.

Mandy glanced down at him, saw he was all right, then looked back at the church wall. The cat had disappeared. She swept her torch along the wall, but there was no sign of it.

'Oh, heck!' James groaned with dismay. 'We only took our eyes off it for a second! Sorry. It was my fault it ran off, wasn't it?'

'Never mind . . .' Mandy stood very still. A really odd feeling was creeping up on her. 'The cat just disappeared, didn't it? As if it just melted into the stone.' She shivered. 'And James,' she said in an unsteady voice, 'I've just realised something else . . .'

'What?' James said crossly. He seemed furious with himself.

'When we saw it, caught in our torchlight,' Mandy whispered, 'it didn't seem to have a shadow . . .'

'But that's impossible,' James gulped. His eyes were wide and a bit scared-looking. 'Are you sure?'

Mandy shrugged, not wanting to believe it herself. It was too creepy! 'Maybe it was a trick of the light . . . or something . . .' she said, trying to find a reasonable explanation. But that trembly feeling inside was telling her that there just wasn't one.

'I don't get it,' James said. 'Is this cat real or isn't it?'

Five

Mr Hope's dark eyebrows rose as Mandy finished telling him all about the mystery cat when she arrived home. Her mum had already left for her yoga class. 'You're sure it's the same cat – the one you've been dreaming about?'

Mandy nodded. 'I'm sure.' Somehow, now that she was at home, sitting in Animal Ark's cosy kitchen, the experience didn't seem so real. But she remembered that awful jolt of shock when she saw the cat. She gave a shiver. 'Something's going on, Dad. But what? I can't work it out.'

Mr Hope came and sat beside her. He put a comforting arm around her shoulders. 'To be honest, I'm not sure, either, love. But there's always an explanation for everything. The trick is to find it.'

Mandy nodded, then gave him a shaky smile. 'But I'd be happy just to find Bathsheba!' She felt better for having told her dad about her and James's scary experience. He might be as puzzled as she was, but he hadn't laughed or told her she was imagining things.

Mr Hope kissed her cheek. 'That's my sensible girl. Come on. Let's start getting supper ready for when your mum gets back from her class. Things always look better on a full stomach.'

Mandy chuckled as she stood up to help her father. 'James would agree with that!' she replied.

'That's because he's got his priorities right. Like me,' Mr Hope joked. 'Don't worry, love. I'm sure we'll get to the bottom of this strange cat business. Like your gran always says – it'll all come out in the wash!'

* * *

'Are you nearly ready, Mandy?' Mrs Hope called up the stairs. 'We'd better be leaving soon if we're going to get to Walton on time.'

It was Sunday morning, and the day of the special service: the congregation of Welford Church was to join that of Walton Church to welcome Reverend Jeavons.

'Just coming, Mum!' Mandy replied, giving her hair a quick brush. She had lain in bed far too long, thinking about Bathsheba and the mystery cat. Since the cat had shown itself to her and James two nights ago, Mandy's dreams had been different. Now, the cat would come out of the shadows, look at her with its piercing blue eyes and call to her. *What* was it trying to tell her? To keep on looking for Bathsheba? Not to give up?

'Reverend Hadcroft is very keen that no one is late!' Mandy's mum called again.

'Yes, Mum, coming!' Mandy raced down the stairs and into the hall to grab her coat and scarf.

The four-wheel drive pulled away slowly from Animal Ark, crunching along the still-frozen ground. In the lane that led up to the Fox and

Goose crossroads, a layer of white frost coated the hedgerows.

It was lucky that she and James were both getting lifts directly to Walton Church this morning, Mandy reflected. Yesterday, being Saturday, they had caught the same bus they sometimes used to get to school. But it didn't run on a Sunday.

There had been no sign of Bathsheba, though. And no sign of the mystery cat either. Perhaps today . . .

'I hope there's a good turn-out for Reverend Jeavons's first service,' Mr Hope said, glancing across at her.

'Me too,' Mandy replied. She felt a bit nervous on Colin's behalf. It would be awful if hardly anyone turned up.

'Don't you worry,' Emily Hope said. 'I expect everyone's keen to get a look at the new vicar. Mrs Ponsonby popped into the surgery yesterday for some of Pandora's special shampoo. She told me that she's helping Reverend Hadcroft organise lifts for people who want to go to the Walton Church service.'

Mandy smiled. Mrs Ponsonby was a large,

bossy woman who was a leading light in Welford's Women's Institute. She doted on Pandora, her spoiled Pekinese. She had another dog too, a young mongrel called Toby.

'Oh, well. With Mrs Ponsonby on the case, there ought to be coachloads arriving for the congregation!' Mr Hope joked.

'Mrs Ponsonby was none too pleased to see Walton's new vicar wearing jeans when she was introduced to him last week,' Mrs Hope informed them, laughing. 'You know how she sets great store by appearances. She told me that she thinks it's improper for a vicar to wear anything but a suit.'

Mandy pulled a face. She thought of Mrs Ponsonby's colourful flowery hats and matching frocks. Even her shoes and glasses matched her outfits. Mandy decided she preferred casual jeans and a sweater any day.

Soon the car reached the outskirts of Welford. On either side of the road, the fields bordered by dry-stone walls looked bleak and wind-blown. Up on the high moors there was a crust of snow.

Mr Hope glanced across at Mandy. 'Did you

have your dream again last night?' he asked.

Mandy nodded.

'It's not upsetting you too much, is it, love?'

Mandy shook her head, thoughtfully. 'No, not really . . .'

Mrs Hope reached over and gave Mandy's hand a reassuring squeeze. 'Mandy's too sensible to be upset by creepy tales,' she said firmly. 'She gets her good sense from my example.'

'Oh, really?' Mr Hope said, with a grin. 'And I thought she got it from mine!'

Mandy chuckled. 'No,' she repeated, more confidently this time, 'I'm not feeling spooked today! But I do wish I knew what was going on!'

'That's my girl,' Mr Hope said, winking at her.

A few minutes later they entered Walton, passing Walton Cottage Hospital and Walton Moor School.

'It looks as if Reverend Hadcroft's efforts to get a good turn-out have paid off,' Mr Hope said as he searched for a parking space near Walton Church. 'There are an awful lot of cars here.'

They found a space in a nearby sidestreet. As

Mandy walked with her parents towards the churchyard, she saw James waiting by the lychgate. 'Hi!' she cried, waving at him.

James waved back. 'Hi, Mr Hope. Hi, Mrs Hope,' he called. 'I thought I'd wait for you here. Mum and Dad are inside.'

Mandy and James fell into step as they all walked towards the main door. She noticed that he seemed to be staring at the building more closely than usual.

'What are you doing?' she asked.

'Checking for interesting angles,' he replied. 'I'm asking permission to come over tomorrow in school lunch-time and take some photographs. Why don't you ask if you can come with me?'

Mandy pulled a face. 'I might do,' she said. She wasn't all that interested in photography, but it would be a good opportunity to search round the churchyard in daylight. 'OK, I'll see if I can get permission,' she said.

'Great!' James said, enthusiastically. 'You can be my assistant.'

'Oh, thanks.' Mandy gave him a narrow look. 'I can hardly wait.'

They had almost reached the stone archway over the front door when Mandy glanced across the churchyard towards the vicarage. She saw Lizzy Jeavons and Daniel come out of the front door and start walking towards them.

'Here come Lizzy and Daniel,' she said to her mum and dad. 'If you hang on a minute, you can meet them.'

Lizzy saw them all waiting. She turned and said something to Daniel and the toddler raised his arm and waved a gloved hand.

'Hi, there!' Lizzy said, as she reached Mandy, James, and Mandy's parents. She smiled at Mandy and James. 'Daniel's been really looking forward to seeing you two again. I told him you might sit with us in church if I asked you nicely.'

'Of course we will!' Mandy said promptly. 'Won't we, James?'

James nodded enthusiastically.

Mandy beamed down at the little boy. 'Hello again, Daniel.'

''Lo.' Daniel peeped out from beneath a woolly hat. His chubby cheeks dimpled as he gave her a toothy grin.

'What a gorgeous little boy!' Emily Hope said. 'How old is he?'

'Two – going on forty!' Lizzy told her wryly. 'He keeps me on my toes. Don't you, Daniel?' she said with a fond smile. 'You must be Mandy's parents. It's nice to meet you both.' She shook hands with each of them in turn. 'Shall we go inside? It's a bit cold to stand out here.'

As they went into the church, Mandy heard her mum say to Lizzy, 'How are you settling in? Mandy told us you're having some decorating work done. That must be a nuisance when you've got a toddler running around.'

Lizzy chuckled. 'Oh, we're managing. Jim and Kevin, our decorators, are very good. Mind you, I could do without the latest complication: they started work on converting the attic into a playroom a couple of days ago. Next thing we knew, we'd got mice everywhere!'

'Oh, dear,' Emily Hope said. 'What a nuisance.'

'Actually, the problem's not too bad,' Lizzy admitted. 'We haven't seen too many mice in the last day or so. Maybe they've found new homes!'

James had heard the conversation too. 'I'm glad I'm not a mouse,' he said. 'You're all tucked up in a cosy nest, then someone comes and turfs you out!'

Mandy nodded. 'Rotten, isn't it?'

As Mandy and James took their seats next to Lizzy and Daniel, Mrs Ponsonby came sailing down the aisle. She was wearing a fluffy blue coat and a matching hat and scarf. Pandora, her Pekinese, was tucked securely beneath her arm, but there was no sign of Toby, her mongrel puppy.

'She must have left Toby at home,' Mandy observed. 'Perhaps she didn't trust him to behave himself.'

'I know the feeling,' James said, grinning.

Mandy giggled. Blackie, James's young black labrador, wasn't the most obedient of dogs . . .

Mandy and James sat with Lizzy and Daniel on one side, and Mandy's and James's parents on the other. When the time arrived for the service to start, the church was almost full. Reverend Hadcroft began the service with a welcome speech. Then he handed over to Reverend Jeavons. Wearing a cassock and spotless white surplice, the new vicar announced the first hymn.

Mandy thought Colin looked very smart. Surely even Mrs Ponsonby would approve.

The sound of singing filled the old church. Mandy could pick out her dad's voice. He sang in the Welford Church choir. After prayers were said, Colin stepped into the pulpit to deliver his first sermon.

'Daddy!' Daniel piped up. 'My daddy!'

There was a ripple of good-natured laughter.

Colin's sermon was great fun. His enthusiasm was infectious. Mandy noticed that even Mrs Ponsonby was nodding approvingly during the bible reading. Everyone stood to sing the final hymn.

Suddenly there was a piercing scream. Mandy saw Mrs Ponsonby jump to her feet and hold Pandora aloft with one hand. The Pekinese licked its lips nervously as it swayed in midair.

'Argh!' she yelled, stamping her feet so that her heels clicked on the stone floor.

'Crikey!' James spluttered. 'She's doing a war dance!'

'More like a flamenco!' Mr Hope said with a wicked glint in his eye.

'Dad!' Mandy almost fell about laughing.

'Help!' Mrs Ponsonby's loud voice boomed out. 'A mouse! It ran over my foot. And there goes another one! This place is *infested*!'

'Uh-oh,' Mandy said. 'No wonder Lizzy hasn't seen many of the mice from her attic.'

'Right,' James agreed. 'They've moved in here. Clever things.'

There was muffled laughter as Mrs Ponsonby jigged about.

'What a fuss,' Mandy said with disgust. 'As if a couple of teeny weeny mice could harm a great big human being.'

But Lizzy Jeavons looked worried. 'Oh, dear,' she said. 'This is awful. Some people are really afraid of mice.'

The service was hurriedly brought to a close. Reverend Jeavons went to the back of the church, ready to shake hands and exchange a few words with each person as they left.

Mandy, James and their parents filed out of their pew and made their way out with Lizzy and Daniel. Mrs Ponsonby barged past importantly in a cloud of strong perfume.

'Ah, Mrs Ponsonby, isn't it? So glad—' Colin got no further.

'I really must protest about the vermin, Vicar!' Mrs Ponsonby launched straight in. 'Mice are filthy things. They spread diseases, you know. And if there are two of them, there are bound to be hundreds more. I got such a shock when I saw them. And my poor Pandora is still in shock . . .'

'I bet she is,' James muttered, 'with Mrs Ponsonby dangling her in the air and screaming right next to her ear.'

Mandy saw that Lizzy Jeavons was trying not to laugh.

'Ah, yes. Thank you for drawing the matter to my attention—' Colin tried to get a word in edgeways, but Mrs Ponsonby was still in full flow.

'It won't do, you know. Mice chew through anything. They'll be running riot. And they breed like . . . well, like mice. And as for their droppings . . .' She gave a shudder that set her fluffy hat trembling. 'You'll just have to get another church cat. And right away! There's absolutely nothing else for it. Bathsheba would have taken care of these vermin . . .'

For once Mandy found herself agreeing with Mrs Ponsonby. If the village bossy-boots managed to persuade Colin to welcome Bathsheba back, she promised herself she'd treat her beloved Pandora to a juicy dog chew!

But Colin was made of sterner stuff and he refused to bow to pressure. 'Thank you, again,' he said firmly. 'You can rest assured that the necessary steps will be taken.'

'Oh, well. All right, Reverend.' A flutter passed over Mrs Ponsonby's plump face. 'I'm glad to hear it. Then I'll bid you good-day. Lovely service, by the way.'

She swept out of the church, her plump little dog held firmly beneath her arm.

'Phew!' Colin said. 'She really knows how to chew a person's ear off!' he sighed. 'She's right, though,' he admitted worriedly, 'I'll have to do something about those mice.'

'Get another cat?' Mandy suggested hopefully.

'I'm afraid there's no chance of that,' Colin replied calmly. 'We'll have to find another solution.'

Mandy looked at James. They both knew what another 'solution' meant. Traps or poison.

'I'll phone the pest control people first thing tomorrow morning,' Colin decided. 'They'll need to come and put down some poison.'

Mandy gulped. It just didn't seem right to put down poison.

'Now, Mandy,' Mrs Hope said gently, seeing her horrified expression. 'Reverend Jeavons must do what he thinks is best.'

Colin shook his head. 'I'm sorry, Mandy. But Mrs Ponsonby's right about one thing. If she's seen two mice there are bound to be dozens more. Traps won't be effective enough. I don't like using poison. But it's likely to be the only sure way to deal with this problem.'

Six

Mandy was dreading seeing the pest control van parked outside the church when she and James passed by on their way to school the following morning.

'Phew!' she said, when she saw only the decorators' van outside the vicarage. 'Maybe Colin's changed his mind about the poison.'

'I wouldn't bet on it,' James said. 'It's probably too early for Colin to have contacted the pest control people yet.'

Kevin was just returning to the van with

Becky and Ben. Mandy and James gave him a friendly wave.

The morning passed quickly. Mandy had two of her favourite subjects. Biology first lesson, then English after break. She'd asked permission to help James take his photographs and met him at the gate at lunch-time.

'Will an hour be enough to take all your photos?' she asked him as they walked the short distance to Walton Church.

James looped the camera case's strap over his shoulder. 'I don't know. I plan to do the ones in the church and the crypt today. I should think we'd be able to come back to do the outside ones tomorrow.'

They didn't waste any time, but went straight to the church's front door.

Mandy tried the handle. 'It's locked.'

'I'll go and see if Colin's over at the vicarage,' James said.

'OK. I'll do a quick check round the churchyard while you're gone,' Mandy replied.

James went off through the trees and Mandy began walking up and down between the rows of gravestones. It was much easier to search in the daylight and she had a clear view across to the hedge.

A few minutes later, she sighed. Nothing – as usual. It had been weeks now since Bathsheba went missing. Mandy reckoned she was one of life's optimists, but even she was starting to think they'd never see the big tabby again.

She saw that Colin was coming over, James at his side. He was carrying a spotlight and a tripod.

'Still at it?' He gave her a friendly grin.

'Yes, but I haven't found anything,' Mandy said glumly.

'Hard luck,' Colin said sympathetically. 'No one can say you haven't tried. Cheer up. Patience is always rewarded.'

'I hope so,' Mandy murmured.

Colin unlocked the church door and led them inside. 'Where do you want to start photographing, James? How about the rood-screen?' he suggested helpfully.

James looked at the carved stone screen that separated the nave from the choir. 'I could do a close-up of the carving. Thanks, Colin. And thanks for letting me borrow your spotlight.'

'No problem,' Colin said. 'I thought you might need it. Especially down in the crypt. Right, I need to make a phone call – then I'll come back and see how you're getting on.'

For the next few minutes Mandy helped James photograph various carvings inside the church. It was awkward adjusting the tripod at first, but she soon got the hang of it.

'We make a great team. The brilliant, talented photographer and his lighting assistant!' James flashed her a sideways look.

Mandy angled the spotlight so that James could get the best shot. 'Don't push your luck!' she said with a grin.

'How are you doing?' Colin reappeared shortly afterwards. 'Ready to go down into the crypt?'

James nodded, then checked his watch. 'Cripes! We've used up over half our lunch-hour already.'

'Better get a move on then,' Colin said with a grin. He picked up the spotlight. 'I'll go and get this set up for you.'

Mandy and James picked up the camera and tripod and followed. At the bottom of the steps, next to the crypt entrance, Mandy almost tripped over a small plastic tray. She looked down as the tray's contents rattled. There was a warning label stuck to the top. A few grains of bright blue powder had spilled over on to the ground nearby.

'Mouse poison,' Mandy whispered flatly. 'And it looks as if the mice have been at it already.'

'Poor things. I expect they think it's a tasty treat,' James whispered back. 'I think it's an awful way to get rid of them. It's a shame that Colin's so against having a cat.'

'I know,' Mandy replied. 'That would be natural pest control. And it would be much kinder to the mice!'

'Come on,' James said. 'It's best not to think about it.'

Mandy knew he was right. But that was easier said than done.

Inside the crypt James got busy. 'I'd really like to photograph the first vicar of Walton's tomb,' he said, checking the camera's display to see how much film he had left. 'His craggy face is really interesting.'

'OK,' Mandy said. She adjusted the light.

James focused on the stern-faced, robed figure, taking photographs from different angles. 'That's good. I've managed to get the whole figure in,' he said. 'These are going to be great!'

One more shot and the camera made a whirring noise as it automatically wound back the used film. 'That's it. I'm out of film,' James said.

'Great timing,' Mandy said. 'We've got about ten minutes to pack up and get back to school.'

As Colin locked up the church behind them, they thanked him again for his help and the loan of his spotlight.

'It was a pleasure,' Colin said. 'Just let me know if you need to borrow the light again.'

'Thanks,' James said. 'Will it be all right if we come back tomorrow lunch-time to photograph the outside?'

'That's fine,' Colin said. 'Tell you what: I'll leave the front door unlocked in case you want to photograph anything else inside the church. I've a couple of parishioners to visit and I might not be back by lunch-time. I wouldn't want you to be locked out.'

'That would be great,' James said. 'Thanks a lot.'

Mandy and James hurried back to school. There was barely time to dash to the cloakroom before lessons started.

'How did it go today at the church?' Emily Hope asked Mandy that evening. 'Did you and James get some good shots?'

'I think so.' Mandy nodded absently. 'We won't really know until James has the film developed.'

Evening surgery was almost over. There were no patients in the waiting-room, so she was helping her mum in the treatment room. They were unpacking dressings and stacking them in a cupboard.

Mrs Hope looked up and smiled. She pushed a strand of her curly red hair behind one ear. 'Photography doesn't compare with looking after animals, does it?'

Mandy grinned at her mum. 'No way!'

Just then the door opened. 'Can you fit in one more patient, Emily?' Jean Knox, the Animal Ark receptionist, asked.

Mrs Hope smiled. 'No peace for the wicked! Yes, of course.'

Kevin the decorator walked through the door, holding Ben and Becky in his arms.

'Kevin! What's wrong?' Mandy said, alarmed.

Mrs Hope laid a hand on Mandy's arm. 'I expect that's what he's here to find out, love.'

Kevin managed a smile for Mandy, but he looked really worried as he put one of the little dogs on the examination table. She noticed that his hands were shaking.

'It's Becky. I think it's her kidneys,' he blurted out. 'She's not a young dog and I know older dogs get kidney failure. And it can be fatal, can't it? – Oh, I don't know what Ben would do without her . . .'

'Now – let's not jump to conclusions,' Mrs Hope said in her gentle, practical way. 'Why don't you tell me Becky's symptoms?'

Kevin gulped, and pushed back his unruly mop of hair. Whimpering, Ben cuddled up close to him. Kevin stroked the little dog absently as he began explaining all in a rush. 'Well, I called in on a chicken farm just outside Welford, after I finished work. Lovely eggs they sell there . . .

Anyway, I let Becky and Ben off their leads for a run about in the yard and I noticed that Becky kept squatting. But she couldn't seem to pass anything . . . if you know what I mean. Just a tiny little drop of wet. So I thought – it could be her kidneys. And you were the nearest vet. So I rushed straight here. Just to be sure, like.'

Mrs Hope nodded calmly. 'Very wise. We can often treat a condition if we catch it early. Let's just have a look at Becky.'

The little Yorkie behaved beautifully as Mrs Hope ran expert fingers over her. 'Hmm. Her bladder is a little inflamed,' she said after a few moments. 'I think that's what's causing the problem. I'd like to do a couple of tests for crystals in her urine. Could you leave her here overnight?'

Kevin blinked. 'I suppose so, if I have to. Only thing is, she's never been away from Ben. Not ever. She'll pine for him something terrible.'

'Ben can stay too, can't he, Mum?' Mandy spoke up without thinking.

'We-ell, we don't encourage it,' Mrs Hope began. 'You know we're pushed for space in the unit.'

'But they could share a cage and I'll take special care of them,' Mandy said persuasively.

Mrs Hope wavered, then she smiled. 'All right. As it's only for one night. But don't think we're making a habit of this, Mandy.'

Looking relieved, Kevin handed Ben to Mandy, then, having nothing left to carry, stuck his hands into his overalls pockets.

He must be in a state, Mandy thought, he hasn't said 'no problem' even once. 'Don't worry. I'll look after them for you,' she assured him. 'Best room in the house and breakfast in bed!'

Kevin smiled weakly. 'Right then. What time shall I call by tomorrow, Mrs Hope?'

'Around lunch-time? I'll have the results by then. OK? And don't worry, I don't think it's all that serious,' Mrs Hope reassured him.

'Really?' Kevin blew out his cheeks. 'Thanks. But I know I won't sleep a wink tonight. Bye, Mandy. Thanks a lot.'

'Right,' Mrs Hope said. 'Let's see about taking a sample of urine, then you can settle in our guests . . .'

* * *

Mandy checked on Becky and Ben before she went to bed and again first thing in the morning. They were curled up together, snug and secure. Two black button noses and two pairs of bright eyes peered out at her from a tangle of chestnut fur.

'Good dogs, you'll be going home soon,' she said, petting them.

'Have you got the tests results yet, Mum?' she asked, popping into the surgery on her way to school.

Mrs Hope smiled. 'Now, how did I know you were going to ask that? Yes, I've got the results. It's as I thought. No crystals in the urine, just a mild bladder infection. I've given Becky an anti-inflammatory injection and put her on a course of tablets. She's going to be fine.'

'So Kevin needn't have fussed about Becky having kidney failure?'

'No. But a fussy owner's a caring owner,' Mrs Hope replied. 'Give me fussy, any day. Unless it's Amelia Ponsonby, of course!'

Mandy giggled. 'Bye. See you later!' She felt all bright and bubbly as she went out of the front door. It always gave her a great feeling to know a sick animal was on the mend. That was one of the reasons why she wanted to be a vet when she was older.

Lunch-time came around and Mandy and James went once again to the churchyard.

Mandy found looking for good angles and shots quite interesting at first. But twenty minutes later, she was starting to find aperture speeds and automatic focus rather boring. Her mind wandered and she began wondering whether Kevin had collected Becky and Ben yet.

James craned his neck, squinting up at the weather vane on the church roof. 'I can't seem to get the focus right for this,' he commented. 'I think I need a more powerful lens.'

'Maybe you should go for something nearer?' Mandy suggested.

'Good thinking,' James trained the camera on one of the decorative arched windows. 'Oh, bother! That's no good either. That whopping great yew tree is casting a shadow...'

'Would you like me to move it out of the way?' Mandy offered helpfully.

'Ha ha, very funny. Let's move farther back. I want to take some shots of the archway over the door.'

'All right.' Mandy sighed. It began to rain again. '*Oh, great!*' she thought. She found herself thinking of warm classrooms and the vending machine in the school corridor that dispensed hot chocolate.

James gave her a pleading look. 'Just a couple more. Then we'll have to stop anyway . . .'

Just then, Mandy heard a faint sound. 'What's that?' she said. 'Listen.'

'What? I didn't hear anything,' James replied, fiddling with his focus.

Mandy tensed. 'There it is again!' A haunting wail floated towards them on the wind. Mandy felt the hairs on the back of her neck stand up. She glanced at James and saw that he'd heard it this time.

'I think . . . it's coming from . . . inside the empty church,' James said. 'It sounds like—'

'The stone-coloured cat . . .' Mandy finished.

The hollow sound, echoing through half a metre of solid York stone, was getting louder. Mandy's imagination went into overdrive. In her mind's eye, she saw lids of stone caskets opening in the crypt as the ancient residents stirred to the unearthly cat's plaintive call.

James hurriedly backed away from the wall and banged into Mandy, who was still fantasising about ghastly happenings in the crypt.

'Argh!' she yelled, almost jumping two metres in the air.

'Sorry!' James said, then knocked the tripod over.

The wind blew stinging drops into Mandy's eyes. She looked away – and caught sight of a movement over by the evergreen hedge. She blinked hard. No – she wasn't imagining it. 'James,' she croaked.

'Hang on a sec, Mandy . . .' James was brushing mud off the tripod. 'I'll get detention for this if I'm not careful!'

But Mandy hardly heard him. She was watching a cat crawling slowly out from under the hedge. First a rounded muzzle and two flattened ears had appeared, now the whole of its skinny body emerged. The cat shook itself, so that its fur stood out in damp spikes. Though

it was thin and bedraggled, and its tabby coat was dark with rainwater and mud, Mandy would have known it anywhere. *Bathsheba!*

'James!' It came out as another dry croak. 'James, look!' Mandy said more loudly, reaching a shaking hand towards him.

'What?' James finally spun round, as Mandy tugged insistently at his coat sleeve. He was just in time to see Bathsheba loping off towards the entrance of the church. James's mouth dropped open. 'Hey! That looked like . . . It couldn't have been . . . could it?'

'Bathsheba! Yes, it was!' Mandy cried.

As if to prove Mandy's words, they heard a familiar wheezy miaow. 'Listen to that!'

'Cripes!' James said, almost dropping his camera. 'It's Bathsheba all right!'

Then, as if in answer to Bathsheba, the plaintive call of the stone-coloured cat rang out again from deep within the church.

'Come on!' Mandy called, hurtling in the same direction as Bathsheba. 'After those cats!'

Seven

As Mandy rounded the bell-tower, she caught a glimpse of Bathsheba dashing awkwardly into the stone entrance porch. She sprinted forward again, James almost at her heels. He was hanging on like mad to his camera case, which was bumping about as he ran.

Moments later, Mandy and James reached the big oak door themselves. It was slightly ajar. Mandy remembered that Colin had said he'd leave it unlocked for them.

The plaintive calling of the stone-coloured cat suddenly drifted away. And, in its place, a different noise began to ring out: a distinctive wheezy miaow.

Mandy and James looked at each other. 'Bathsheba!' they said together. They dragged the heavy oak door fully open and went inside.

The anxious miaows and wails seemed to fill the church. Mandy grabbed James's arm. 'Let's go slowly,' she warned. 'We have to be careful not to alarm her in the distressed state she's in. Don't make any sudden movements or noises.'

James nodded. 'I bet I can guess where she'll be,' he said. He pointed in the direction of the crypt steps.

They walked slowly over there, softly calling Bathsheba's name. The breathy miaowing seemed to grow even more urgent.

The top of the crypt steps came into view and, sure enough, a small dark shape was crouching at the top of the steps.

'Bathsheba! Hello, girl!' Mandy called softly. As soon as the tabby saw Mandy and James, she opened her mouth wide and gave another plaintive howl. *Miaow-ow-ow!*

Mandy couldn't stop herself from hurrying over. She was anxious to find out if the tabby was all right. 'Oh, you clever girl,' she said softly. 'You've remembered your favourite place.' Her heart turned over. Bathsheba was so thin and her coat was full of burrs.

'Poor thing,' said James. 'She looks half-starved.'

Bathsheba pushed herself awkwardly up to a standing position. Then, looking straight at Mandy and James, the pupils enormous in her green eyes, she flicked her tail and darted away, down the crypt steps.

'Oh no!' Mandy cried. 'She's running away from us! But she needs help!'

They hurried down the steps after her. The crypt entrance was in shadow. The stone angels guarding the archway seemed to loom out at them.

And there, on the cold stone floor, was Bathsheba – crouching beside a small, still form.

Mandy drew in her breath sharply. 'Oh, no! James – look! It's little Daniel!' She threw herself down beside the unconscious toddler, her heart pounding. 'It looks like he might have fallen down the steps!'

'We'd better not move him, in case he's broken something,' James said, white-faced. 'You stay here; I'll go and get help.' He turned to run back up the steps.

'Wait a minute!' Mandy called. There was an upturned plastic tray lying near Daniel's outstretched arm. She picked it up and shook it. Almost empty. A couple of grains of blue-dyed powder fell on to the floor. She remembered kicking the tray the day before. Then it had been almost full. A horrible suspicion crept over her.

She bent right down to get a closer look at the toddler's face. There were dark blue stains round his mouth. 'Daniel's not unconscious because he's fallen down the steps and knocked himself out,' she cried, 'It's because he's eaten mouse poison!'

James and Mandy kneeled beside Daniel's unconscious form. They looked at each other in dismay.

'If nothing's broken, it should be OK to move him,' decided James. 'I'll push, you pull.'

Mandy nodded. Together, they rolled Daniel over on to his back.

'Crikey! He looks awful.' James mouth was tight with concern. 'Is he . . . is he still breathing?'

'I'm . . . not sure.' Although Mandy's hands shook, she felt herself grow calm. She remembered all the times she had watched her mum and dad deal with animal emergencies. She had to help Daniel.

Quickly, she checked to see if Daniel was breathing. 'Yes,' she replied in relief. 'But it's rapid and shallow, which I don't think is good.' She scooped Daniel up in her arms. 'There's no time to waste!'

James ran ahead up the steps. 'We'll take it in turns to carry him,' he said. 'Tell me when you want me to take over.'

Panting, Mandy nodded. For such a little boy, Daniel was surprisingly heavy. She plunged on, ignoring the burning in her leg muscles. Daniel's blond head sagged against her as she ran up the nave. A sudden thought struck her.

'James!' she said, without relaxing her stride. 'Can you bring what's left of the poison, please?

The hospital will need to know what Daniel's swallowed.'

'Right! Good thinking!' James dashed back down to the crypt.

Mandy didn't stop to wait for him. She clutched the toddler to her chest and rushed out of the church and towards the vicarage.

As the wind and rain swirled around her, Daniel stirred and gave a soft moan.

'*Oh, please,*' Mandy prayed to herself, her eyes pricking with tears. '*Please let us have found him in time!*'

'Do you want me to take Daniel?' James asked anxiously, as he caught her up. Mandy nodded. Daniel's weight was beginning to make her arms really ache.

'Mandy! James!' a voice called.

Mandy gave a sigh of relief. Lizzy Jeavons was rushing up to them.

'Oh, thank goodness you've found Daniel,' Lizzy said. 'I've been searching for him everywhere . . . What's happened, has he fallen over . . .?' She broke off, suddenly realising that something was badly wrong.

'He's eaten mouse poison,' Mandy said

urgently. 'Look – you can see the blue dye round his mouth.'

'Mandy thinks he ate almost a whole tray,' James put in.

'Poison? Oh no!' Lizzy gasped in shock, reaching out to take her son. 'Give him to me now, Mandy love. Has he said anything at all?'

Mandy shook her head. 'He was unconscious when we found him. I checked his breathing. But we didn't know what else to do . . .'

'Don't worry. You did just the right thing,' Lizzy said. She was taking deep breaths, fighting to keep calm. 'There's no time to call an ambulance. We'll take him straight to hospital. Would you two please run ahead and ask Colin to get the car ready?'

'Right.' Mandy and James dashed towards the vicarage.

'I thought he wasn't going to be back until after lunch-time,' James said.

'He must have finished his parish visits early!' Mandy took a short cut across a flowerbed. 'Good thing for Daniel!'

The back door of the vicarage was unlocked and they shot straight in. Colin was sitting at a table in the unfinished kitchen. He looked up from working at his computer.

'Whoa there, you two! Where's the fire?' He dragged his fingers through his thick sandy hair and gave them his usual friendly grin.

'Lizzy needs you to get the car ready!' Mandy burst out at once. 'Daniel needs to go to hospital! He's eaten mouse poison!'

'Oh no! How on earth did he get inside the church?'

'The door was open when we arrived,' Mandy said.

'But I'm sure I latched it . . .' Colin said, looking puzzled. 'Or, at least, I think I did. I can't remember now. Oh, this is terrible . . .'

He jumped to his feet, jerked his car keys from a wall hook, and hurled himself through the open back door.

Mandy and James followed him outside. Colin had the car door open and the engine running, just as Lizzy pelted down the garden path holding Daniel.

Seconds later, Lizzy and Daniel were clambering into the back seat. Mandy ran forward and closed the car door behind them.

'Oh, I almost forgot.' At the last moment, James thrust the almost empty poison container in through the open car window. 'We thought you might need this.'

Colin put the tray on the front passenger seat. 'Thanks, you two,' he said in a shaky voice. 'Will you be all right here?'

'Yes. You just go.' Mandy searched for the right words. 'I hope Daniel will be OK.'

Colin managed a bleak smile. 'So do I.'

There was no more time to talk. The car sped away towards the hospital.

Mandy felt her legs almost give way. She staggered into the vicarage kitchen and sat down.

James sat down heavily too. He was white as a sheet. 'Do you think Daniel will be all right?' he asked.

'I don't know,' Mandy said worriedly. 'But the hospital will know what to do . . .' Suddenly she sat up straight. 'Bathsheba!' she cried. 'What about Bathsheba? She might still be in the church!'

James jumped up. 'Let's go and find out!'

The tabby was in her favourite place, at the top of the crypt steps. 'Look at her. All curled up asleep,' Mandy said with relief.

One of Bathsheba's ears twitched, then her eyes opened. She lifted her head and blinked in confusion. Mandy kneeled on the steps and began stroking the cat's broad head. 'Hello, old girl,' she breathed. 'Welcome home.'

Bathsheba managed a weak, wheezy purr, but a tremor ran over her thin body.

'Oh, my goodness,' Mandy sighed. 'Look at her!'

'Poor old thing.' James frowned, looking puzzled. 'She seemed all right a few minutes ago, but she seems really weak now.'

Mandy became all action. She slipped her hands beneath Bathsheba and gently lifted her. She felt the tabby trying to stand up, but her legs seemed all wobbly. 'Come on – let's take her into the vicarage. I'm going to phone Animal Ark.' For the second time that day, Mandy found herself hurrying for help.

Emily Hope listened in silence as Mandy finished explaining. '. . . so we went back to fetch Bathsheba, after Colin and Lizzy took Daniel to hospital, and now she's here, with us, in the vicarage. She's really thin and weak.'

'Right,' her mum said. 'Thank goodness Daniel's getting expert treatment. Sounds like you and James have been pretty busy! You two stay there. Your dad's taking afternoon surgery and I'm on call, so I'll come straight over. I'll be about ten minutes.'

'OK, Mum.' Mandy put the phone down. 'Mum will be here soon,' she said to James. Mandy looked down at Bathsheba, curled up on James's lap.

'She's so thin,' he said. 'You can feel her ribs and all the bumps on her backbone. And her coat's full of burrs . . . But *phew*!' James wrinkled his nose. 'She smells a bit too!'

'She can't help it,' Mandy said defensively. Mandy began combing the hooked seeds and bits of twig out of the cat's fur with her fingers. But it was no use. Bathsheba needed a full grooming job. Comb, brush, bath – the works.

'Poor girl,' James crooned, rubbing the cat under her chin. 'I wonder when she last had a good meal.'

Mandy shook her head. She frowned. 'You know what puzzles me?'

'No, what?' James asked.

'Why, after all these weeks, did Bathsheba come back when she did?' Mandy said. 'How did she know help was needed?'

James looked a bit uncomfortable. 'Well, there is one possibility,' he said. 'but it's a bit of a creepy one . . .'

'Go on,' Mandy said, curiously.

'Perhaps the stone-coloured cat called her back,' he suggested.

* * *

A few minutes later Mrs Hope drew up outside in her four-wheel drive. She came dashing into the house, carrying a cardboard pet carrier. 'Are you two all right?' she asked at once, putting the carrier on the table. 'It must have given you both quite a shock, finding Daniel like that.'

Mandy nodded, suddenly close to tears and very glad to see her mum. 'It did. He looked so small, lying all crumpled up on the floor like that. His little face was all white and pinched.'

Mrs Hope gave her a cuddle. 'Try not to think about that. He's in good hands now. It's up to the hospital now, OK?' She turned and smiled at James. 'You two did really well. Your quick thinking could make all the difference. Poor Colin and Lizzy. They must be frantic with worry. I only hope the little lad will be all right.'

'Me too,' Mandy and James both replied.

'Right,' Mrs Hope said, becoming all practical. 'Let's have a look at this feline casualty. This one, I *can* do something about.' She bent down and gently picked up Bathsheba.

Mandy watched as her mum examined the cat, searching for signs of wounds or infections.

'Hmm. She's just skin and bone. Looks like she's been living rough,' Emily Hope judged. 'Probably needs worming before anything else.'

'But will she be OK?' Mandy asked.

'I can't see any obvious signs of infection. But I'll give her a more thorough examination once I get her back to Animal Ark,' Mrs Hope replied. She gave Bathsheba a friendly pat. 'Up you come, girl,' she said, lifting her into the pet carrier.

'Can we come back to Animal Ark with you?' Mandy asked. She wanted to make sure that Bathsheba was given the all-clear. Then she planned to get her settled in comfortably. After her ordeal, the cat deserved the warmest spot in the residential unit and a dish of food.

'Aren't you and James supposed to be somewhere else?' her mum asked, with a wry grin. 'Like school? I don't suppose either of you thought to telephone and explain your absence?'

Mandy shook her head. 'There wasn't time. It was an emergency.'

'Hmm,' Mrs Hope murmured. 'Even so—'

'Uh-oh!' James clapped his hands to his

mouth. 'I've just realised. I bet there was a fuss when we didn't show up for afternoon registration!'

Mandy groaned. 'Oh, yes. I didn't think about that either. They've probably got search parties out for us and everything!'

'Dog-teams, snow sleds, choppers . . .' James took things one step further.

Mrs Hope chuckled. 'Hardly! But I expect the school is getting a bit concerned. I'll give them a ring and explain why you'll be returning late.'

'Do we have to go back?' Mandy pleaded, her blue eyes wide. 'It's only for a couple of hours.'

'Yes, you do,' Mrs Hope said firmly. 'I'm going back to Animal Ark – alone. And we'll have to lock up the vicarage behind us. So you can't stay here.'

Mandy sighed. Sometimes she might be able to get round her soft-hearted dad, but her mum was a different matter. Mrs Hope was gentle and caring, but she knew when to be firm.

Mrs Hope went off to make the phone call. She returned a couple of minutes later. 'All sorted,' she said. 'I spoke to your Head. He was very interested to hear about your rescue mission. He seems to think you're both heroes.'

Mandy groaned softly. She looked at James, imagining some kind of awful show-and-tell session in front of the whole school. How embarrassing!

'Do you want to bring Bathsheba out to the car, Mandy?' Mrs Hope asked. 'I'd better get back to the surgery and see to her right away. I'm likely to get called out at any time. And it's Simon's day off.' Simon was the practice nurse.

As Mandy picked up the pet carrier, Bathsheba gave a low, plaintive wail. Mandy slipped her hand inside the carrier and stroked her reassuringly. 'I'll come and see you the second I get back from school,' she promised.

They all trooped out to the drive. Mrs Hope hung back a moment to make sure the vicarage was locked, then she stowed the carrier in the back of the car.

'Bye, love,' she said, to Mandy, kissing her cheek. 'See you after school. Bye, James.'

'Bye, Mrs Hope. And thanks,' James said politely.

'Meet you here later?' James said to Mandy,

at the school gate. 'I'll come back to Animal Ark with you and check up on Bathsheba. At least we won't have to go prowling about in that creepy churchyard any more!'

'Oh, yes!' Mandy nodded, brightening. 'There's no need, now.'

Luckily the conversation with the Head was brief and less embarrassing than Mandy had imagined. She and James went off to their separate classes.

Mandy took out her maths book and spread it open on her desk. But she knew there was no way she was going to be able to concentrate. All she could think about was Bathsheba: returned – but now homeless.

Eight

'Hi, Jean. Where's Mum?' Mandy asked Animal Ark's receptionist, the moment she and James got through the surgery door.

'Hello, you two!' Jean Knox said cheerfully. 'Your mum's just got back from one of those isolated farms up on the high moor. I think she's in the unit.'

'Thanks,' Mandy said. 'We'll go straight through.'

'Busy afternoon, Mum?' Mandy asked. 'Jean said you'd been called out.'

Mrs Hope was wearing her white lab coat.

She nodded. 'A ewe miscarried twin lambs. They didn't survive, I'm afraid. But I've checked the mother over and she'll be fine.'

'Oh.' Mandy hated to hear of any animal dying. But she knew it was fairly common for sheep to miscarry. Their next lambs were almost always all right.

'On a brighter note, your friend Kevin's been and collected his Yorkies,' her mum continued. 'He was over the moon when I told him Becky was going to be fine.'

'That's great,' Mandy said. 'Now all we have to do is get Bathsheba well. Can James and I see her?'

Mrs Hope nodded. 'I've put her out the back in the quarantine room. Just for a couple of days.'

'Has she got something catching, Mrs Hope?' James asked.

'I don't think so,' Mrs Hope replied. 'But she could be incubating something. It's best not to take chances. Stray cats can pick up all kinds of things.'

Bathsheba was curled up on a blanket in her heated cage. As soon as she saw Mandy and

James she gave one her special loud miaows.

'She recognises us!' James said.

'Of course she does!' Mandy said, opening the door and giving Bathsheba a cuddle.

Mrs Hope smiled. 'She's a lot more comfortable now. But she's badly undernourished. She's going to need to eat little and often until she puts some weight on.'

'Did you have to give her any treatment?' Mandy asked.

'I've given her a vitamin injection and a worming tablet,' Mrs Hope replied. 'And she's eaten a dish of kitten food. But that's all. It's amazing really that she doesn't seem to have caught even a snuffle.'

'That's wonderful!' Mandy said happily. She'd been imagining all kinds of complications. 'So, all she needs is loads of food!'

'And TLC!' James said. 'My dad says that's the best medicine.'

'He's right.' Mrs Hope went over to a sink and washed her hands with antibacterial fluid. 'You two can stop worrying now. Bathsheba's going to be fine.'

'Except that she's homeless,' Mandy said

quietly. She gave Bathsheba a final cuddle, before closing the cage door.

'Hello, you two. I thought you'd be in here.' Adam Hope came into the unit. He was followed by Reverend Jeavons. 'I met Colin here on the drive. He's got something to tell you.'

Colin was beaming. 'Daniel's going to be fine. He's a bit groggy and he has a tummy-ache so they're keeping him in overnight, but only for observation. Lizzy's staying with him, so I've come home to fetch a few things for her. I thought I'd just pop over and give you two the good news.'

'That's just great. Isn't it, James?' Mandy said.

'Yeah. It's brilliant,' James said, smiling.

'It certainly is,' Emily Hope agreed. 'Daniel's a very lucky little boy.'

'It was a close call, though,' Colin said seriously. 'I feel just terrible about leaving the church door unlatched. Daniel was obviously able to push it open. I'd never have forgiven myself if the worst had happened . . .' He broke off to run his hands through his hair. 'Anyway – luckily for all of us, the doctor reckons Mandy and James found Daniel just in time. Another half an hour and it might have been too late.'

Mandy suddenly felt cold all over. She hardly dared think about what might have happened.

'And your quick thinking, suggesting we take along the remains of the poison, really helped,' Colin informed them. 'The doctor was able to identify the type of poison and give Daniel the necessary treatment immediately.'

'That was Mandy's idea,' James said generously.

'Well, it was a real brainwave.' Colin smiled down at her. 'Thanks a lot, Mandy. And you, James. Lizzy and I are very, very grateful to you both. You'll never know just how much.'

James blushed to the roots of his hair. 'That's OK,' he said.

Mandy shifted her feet. She always got embarrassed when people thanked her. 'Anyone would have done the same,' she murmured.

'I'm not sure they would have,' Colin said. 'In that situation, most people would have panicked. And that includes a few adults I can think of!'

'Our Mandy's got a level head on her

shoulders,' Mr Hope said proudly, ruffling his daughter's fair hair.

Colin folded his arms and leaned back against the shelf. Behind him, in her cage, Bathsheba curled up and went to sleep. 'One thing still puzzles me though. How did you two manage to find Daniel? You'd finished taking photographs in the crypt, hadn't you, James?'

James nodded.

'We weren't planning to go anywhere near the crypt,' Mandy explained. 'We only went down there after Bathsheba. We saw her running into the church after that strange stone-coloured cat.'

'We guessed she'd have gone to her favourite place – and there she was,' James continued. 'But she wouldn't come when we called her – she ran down the steps leading to the crypt, so we followed her . . . and found Daniel.'

'So you see,' Mandy said slowly, 'it wasn't me and James who saved Daniel's life. It was Bathsheba. She *led* us to him!'

Colin shook his head slowly. 'It's an incredible story. I don't know what Lizzy's going to make of it when she hears about this.'

'She'll probably be as puzzled as the rest of us,' Mr Hope said, scratching his head. 'I haven't got the foggiest about all this.'

'But it's all true, Dad,' Mandy said. 'Isn't it, James?'

James nodded. '*Strange*, but true,' he corrected in a hollow voice.

Colin scratched his head again, at a loss. 'Well, I'd better be going,' he said. 'I promised Lizzy I wouldn't be long. I said I'd take her some sandwiches and a Thermos of soup. Hospitals aren't exactly known for their good food!'

'I'd better go home now, too,' James said. 'Supper will be ready.'

'I'll drop you home if you like,' Colin offered. 'It's on the way.'

Mandy walked with James and Colin to the front door.

'Do you think it would it be OK if Daniel comes to see Bathsheba?' Colin said to her, pausing in the doorway. 'I'm sure Lizzy would like to visit her too, especially after what she's done for us.'

'Course it's OK!' Mandy said. 'Mum and Dad won't mind. They can come any time.'

'Thanks,' Colin said. 'Thanks again, for everything. Bye, now. See you soon.'

Mandy was thoughtful as she went into the kitchen. Her dad was clearing the newspapers from the kitchen table, while her mum set about getting supper ready.

'Uh-oh!' Mr Hope said, with a twinkle in his eye. 'I know that look!'

'What do you mean?' Mandy said innocently.

'You're hatching something, Mandy Hope. Out with it!'

Mandy grinned. 'It's nothing really. I was . . . er . . . just wondering what was going to happen to Bathsheba now. I mean – she can't go back to the vicarage. We'll have to try and rehome her, won't we?'

'I thought that might be it.' Mr Hope sighed. 'I expect you're racking your brains trying to think who might adopt her? You've done all you can for her, love. We'll phone one of the cat rescue organisations and let them take care of it, OK?'

'I suppose so.' Mandy sank into a chair and cupped her chin in her hands. Poor Bathsheba. She deserved a good home after all she had been through. But she was going to have to stay in a pen in a cattery until someone adopted her.

'Tell you what.' Mrs Hope looked up from chopping carrots. 'How about if we allow Bathsheba to stay with us in the cottage until she's fully recovered? But only until then, OK? That will give us time to organise rehoming her.'

'You mean it?' Mandy jumped up. She went over and gave her mum a huge hug. 'Thanks a million, Mum. Wait until I tell James!'

It wasn't an ideal solution. But she was going to make the most out of having Bathsheba around – if only for a short while.

A couple of days later, Bathsheba was ready to leave the unit. Mandy and James were getting her settled into a box in the kitchen for the rest of her stay.

Mandy folded a piece of old blanket and put it into a small cardboard box. 'There. That makes a cosy bed. What do you think, Bathsheba?'

The tabby was crouched on the red-patterned

rug. She looked up at the sound of her name, then trotted over to investigate the box.

James watched her sniffing the cardboard and nosing the blanket. 'She's scent-marking. I think she likes it.'

Mandy, meanwhile, spread newspaper on the stone floor, then forked cat food into a bowl. As soon as Bathsheba smelled food, she forgot about her bed. She padded straight over and began eating.

'Gosh! She's scoffed the lot already!' James said a couple of minutes later.

Bathsheba licked her lips, then sat down on the rug and began washing herself meticulously. She was lying full-length on the rug when the door opened and Mr Hope poked his head into the room.

'Visitors for you,' he announced.

'Hi, you two.' Lizzy came into the room, holding Daniel by the hand. 'We came to say thanks to you. And to Bathsheba! As you can see – Daniel's fine now!'

'Hi, Lizzy. Hi, Daniel!' James and Mandy replied, delighted to see that the toddler looked none the worse for his experience.

Daniel gave them a sunny smile. ' 'Lo,' he said. But as soon as he spotted Bathsheba, his mouth dropped open in wonder. He pointed a chubby finger at her. 'Look! Pussy cat!'

Mandy and James laughed as Daniel went over and sat on the rug beside Bathsheba. He stretched out his hand and began softly stroking her head. Bathsheba purred, enjoying the attention.

'Ah,' Daniel murmured. 'Nice pussy cat.' He stroked her ears gently, then put his arms round Bathsheba and laid his cheek against her tabby coat.

'Oh dear.' Lizzy looked worried as Daniel stretched out on the rug beside the cat. 'I don't know if that's a good idea.'

She took a step forward, ready to rescue Bathsheba from Daniel's affectionate embrace. But she needn't have worried. Bathsheba, purring loudly, snuggled up close to the toddler and closed her eyes.

'Look at that,' Mandy said, in amazement. 'She really seems to have taken to him.'

'The feeling seems to be mutual,' Lizzy said with a chuckle. 'I think Daniel's in love!'

'It's a shame that Colin's so against having a cat, isn't it?' James said.

'Walton Church just won't be the same without Bathsheba,' Mandy said wistfully.

Lizzy looked uncomfortable. 'We'd love to adopt Bathsheba,' she said. '*Especially* after what she did for us . . . I'm sure that if it wasn't for Colin's allergy, he might think differently, but . . .' She lapsed into an awkward silence.

Mandy nodded sadly. But something else was niggling at the back of her mind. Something important, concerning Bathsheba. If only she could remember what it was . . .

'I wondered if you'd both like to come to tea at the vicarage,' Lizzy said, changing the subject. 'It's by way of a thank you, for all you've done.'

'We'd love to, wouldn't we, James?' Mandy said.

James nodded. 'You bet!'

'That's settled then,' Lizzy said. 'How about Saturday?'

'Fine,' Mandy replied. 'I'll just have to check with Mum—' Suddenly she jumped up. 'That's it! I've remembered!'

James and Lizzy gaped as Mandy waved her

hands about with excitement. 'Lizzy, I've got something to tell you. If I'm right it could solve our problem . . .'

Nine

Mandy began her explanation. 'The other day, Colin was so excited about Daniel being OK that he didn't notice Bathsheba. He stood right next to her cage in the unit for about ten minutes. And he didn't sneeze once!'

'Oh, yes . . . That's right!' James confirmed.

Lizzy looked thoughtful. 'You know – this could make all the difference.'

'You mean – Colin might consider adopting Bathsheba?' Mandy asked hopefully, her eyes shining.

'I'm not sure,' Lizzy replied. 'He still might

not want to risk having a cat around. I think we need a plan to persuade him to give it a try. I have an idea, but I'll need some help.'

'We'll help, won't we, James?' Mandy said promptly.

James nodded. 'Of course!'

'Right then,' Lizzy said, rubbing her palms together. 'How about if, on Saturday, you and James bring Bathsheba with you. I'll make sure Colin's busy, so he doesn't see you arrive. We'll put the pet carrier somewhere in the room, but out of sight.'

'That's brilliant!' Mandy said. 'Then we'll know for certain whether Colin's allergic to her!'

'Exactly!' Lizzy said. 'And if everything's OK, we'll bring Bathsheba out. I don't think there'll be any objection to us adopting her after that!'

James was grinning from ear. 'I just hope it works!'

'Me too!' Mandy said with feeling.

'That's settled then.' Lizzy went over to Daniel, who was still curled up with Bathsheba. 'Time to go now, Daniel. Mummy has to do some shopping on the way home. Say bye-bye to Bathsheba.'

Daniel's bottom lip quivered ominously. 'Want to stay with pussy cat!'

'I know you do. We'll see her again very soon,' Lizzy promised. 'But she needs to sleep now. Come on, little man.'

Rather reluctantly, Daniel stood up. 'Night-night, pussy cat.'

'He misses that creamy-grey cat that used to visit us,' Lizzy observed. 'He still looks out for it. But it seems to have stopped coming now. Anyway, see you on Saturday. How about four o'clock?'

'We'll be there,' Mandy and James said.

Lizzy and Daniel made their way out. As soon as Mandy had seen them off, she dashed back indoors. 'I've got to tell Mum and Dad about our plan!'

Mr and Mrs Hope chuckled when they heard the details. 'Well I never! That's what I call devious,' Adam Hope said.

'No, Dad,' Mandy insisted. 'It's called . . . gentle persuasion! I reckon Bathsheba's as good as adopted!'

'Hmm.' Emily Hope gave her daughter a steady look. 'I just hope you and James aren't counting your chickens . . .'

On Saturday morning, Mandy ate a hurried breakfast. As soon as she'd finished she dashed along to the residential unit to do her chores.

She mopped floors, cleaned out cages and changed water in dishes. It might not be interesting or exciting work, but it had to be done.

'Finished!' she announced an hour or so later, as she bounded back into the kitchen.

'Do I take it you have the rest of the day all planned out?' her dad guessed, as she tugged off her wellies and stood them on some newspaper.

'Yep! James is calling round for lunch. Then we're going to get Bathsheba ready to go to the vicarage.'

'Ah, yes. It's delivery-day, isn't it?' Mr Hope smiled. 'I'll drop you at the vicarage if you like. What time are you going?'

Mandy told him. 'We have to be on time. Lizzy's going to make sure that Colin's occupied when we arrive.'

'Right, ma'am.' Mr Hope clicked his heels and performed a mock salute. 'Your chauffeur will be standing by!'

Mandy searched for a grooming brush, then went into the sitting-room and curled up on the sofa. Bathsheba jumped straight on to her lap. As Mandy brushed her, the tabby purred contentedly.

'Your coat's looking much better already,' Mandy murmured. 'And James can't complain – you smell lovely now!'

Bathsheba made a 'brup' sound of approval. Mandy chuckled, rubbing the cat behind her ears. Part of her felt sad that she wouldn't be looking after the tabby for much longer. But if Lizzy's plan worked, Bathsheba would be back in her rightful place and she and James would be able to go and visit her.

James arrived, just before lunch-time. He took a package out of his coat pocket. 'I collected my photos on the way over.'

'Oh, great,' Mandy said. 'Let's go and show them to Mum and Dad.'

Emily Hope was making lunch. 'It's only tomato soup and sandwiches as I expect you'll be having a fair amount of food at the vicarage.'

'That sounds great. Thanks, Mrs Hope,' James sat down and took his photos out of their envelope. He passed them round in turn.

'These are really good,' Mr Hope said, looking at the different views of the church. 'I shouldn't be surprised if you get top marks for the art project.'

James blushed and fiddled with his glasses. 'I hope so. But it wasn't just me. Mandy helped.'

'And if you hadn't been taking photos, we would never have noticed Bathsheba running into the church after the stone-coloured cat!' Mandy said.

'Oh, yes. Whatever happened to that other cat?' Mrs Hope put bowls of soup on the table.

Mandy shrugged. 'I don't know. Lizzy says she hasn't seen it for a while. And I haven't dreamed about it for ages now – not since Bathsheba came back . . .' she said, thoughtfully.

Mr Hope winked at her. 'I've a feeling we've seen the last of the mystery cat.'

* * *

'I'm just going to feed Bathsheba before we leave,' Mandy said, a couple of hours later. 'She usually falls asleep the moment she's finished eating.'

'That's a good idea,' James said. 'Then we won't have to worry about her miaowing and giving the game away.'

Once they were ready to go, Mandy lifted the tabby into the carrier. Bathsheba settled down at once and tucked her nose into her paws.

'Right then. All set?' Mr Hope came into the room, jangling his car keys.

James nodded, pulling on his coat. 'I think I'll take my photos. Lizzy and Colin might like to see them.'

There wasn't a sound from Bathsheba during the journey to Walton. Mandy felt nervous and excited both at once. The Land-rover drew up in front of the vicarage and Mandy and James got out.

'Enjoy yourselves – and good luck!' Mr Hope said. 'I hope the plan works. Give me a ring if you need a lift back.'

'Thanks, Dad.' Mandy said. 'I've got my fingers and toes crossed!'

The vicarage door opened and Lizzy appeared. 'Come on in. Colin's upstairs with Daniel.'

She led Mandy and James into the kitchen. She had been cooking and the whole room smelled wonderful.

Mandy saw that new cupboards and shelves had been fitted, but the decorating wasn't finished yet. A pile of long wooden planks was stacked against one wall.

'I thought we'd tuck Bathsheba away behind this wood,' Lizzy said.

'OK.' Mandy put the pet carrier in position.

Lizzy took Mandy and James's coats. 'Make yourselves at home. I'll just go and tell Colin and Daniel you're here.'

Daniel came running into the kitchen a few moments later, followed by Colin, wearing jeans and a bright red sweater.

'Hello there. Nice to see you two again!' he said warmly. 'I hope you've got good appetites. Lizzy's cooked enough for an army!'

'Where pussy cat?' Daniel said expectantly,

looking round with a big smile on his face.

'Mandy and James have left Bathsheba at Animal Ark,' Colin explained to his son.

Daniel frowned and shook his head. 'Want see pussy cat!'

Uh-oh. Mandy threw James an anxious glance. She sensed a tantrum building. If Daniel insisted on searching the room for Bathsheba, he'd give the game away.

Lizzy stepped forward quickly and swept up the toddler. She plonked Daniel in his high-chair and gave him a little pile of grated cheese. 'You and cats!' she said, affectionately, kissing his cheek. 'That's all you think about!'

Distracted, Daniel giggled and began delicately picking at the cheese and eating it strand by strand.

'Phew! That was close,' James said, just loud enough for Mandy to hear.

'Right. Everyone ready to eat?' Lizzy began putting food on the table.

Mandy and James offered to help. So far, so good, Mandy thought as she set out plates. Not a single sneeze from Colin.

There was macaroni cheese and grilled tomatoes, followed by scones and spicy carrot cake. Lizzy certainly could cook.

'That was lovely, thanks, Lizzy,' Mandy said, half an hour later.

'Yep, it was great,' James agreed. 'I couldn't eat another thing.'

'It must have been good then,' Colin joked.

James, shy as usual, reddened. 'I've brought my photos with me. Would you like to see them?'

'I'd love to,' Colin said. 'In a moment, though, if that's OK, James. I've something to tell you all first.'

Lizzy looked at her husband in surprise. 'What's this, Colin? Have you been keeping secrets?'

'Who, me?' Colin grinned. 'Never. But I've come to a decision and I thought I'd wait until today to tell you all. It's about Bathsheba—'

'Oh.' Mandy held her breath. *Now what?*

'I want us to adopt her,' Colin was saying. 'After what she did for us, she deserves to have a home here. I know what I've said in the past, but I'm prepared to put up with the sneezing and snuffles—'

'But you won't have to—' Mandy burst out, before she could stop herself.

'Uh-oh,' James said. 'That's torn it!'

Colin looked from one to the other. 'What do you mean?'

'Oh, this is wonderful!' Lizzy started laughing. 'Looks like the cat's out of the bag!'

Mandy and James began to laugh too.

Colin scratched his head, looking bemused. 'Would anyone like to tell me what's going on?'

'Why don't we show him?' Mandy said, jumping up. She fetched the carrier and brought it over to Colin.

Colin's jaw dropped as Mandy took Bathsheba out and put her on the floor.

'Look!' Daniel gave a shriek of delight and clapped his hands. 'Cat! Cat!'

'Just a minute,' Colin said. 'Has that cat been in the room since you arrived?'

Mandy nodded. 'We brought her with us.'

'But . . . I'm not sneezing. My eyes aren't running . . .'

Lizzy chuckled. 'No. Because you're not allergic to Bathsheba! Mandy said you weren't.

But we wanted to be sure. We were going to try to persuade you to adopt Bathsheba, but we didn't need to.'

'No!' Mandy said. 'You'd already decided to do that – all by yourself!'

Colin looked as if he couldn't believe it. 'Hang on . . .' he looked at Mandy, James and Lizzy's innocent faces. 'If I'm not mistaken, there's been some kind of a conspiracy going on here! OK, you lot. Time to own up!'

Two minutes later Colin knew everything. 'Ha, ha, ha!' he spluttered. 'Oh, this is priceless. You all ganged up on me, you wretches'

Lizzy went over and gave him a hug. 'You big softie,' she said. 'You really would have put up with your allergy, wouldn't you, so we could adopt Bathsheba?'

'A man's gotta do what a man's gotta do,' Colin said in a Texan drawl.

'That's the worst impression I've ever heard!' Lizzy giggled. 'I wouldn't give up the day job, if I were you!'

Mandy felt like jumping for joy. Their brilliant plan had backfired, but everything had worked out for the best. Bathsheba had a home for life!

Daniel was stroking the cat's head, an expression of pure delight on his little face. Bathsheba was basking in the attention. Her wheezy purr seemed to fill the room. Lizzy poured some milk in a saucer and put it down for Bathsheba.

'Just for a special treat,' she said. 'Cats shouldn't have milk very often. It isn't good for them, is it, Mandy?'

Mandy smiled and shook her head. She could see that Lizzy and Colin were going to be caring and responsible owners. And Bathsheba would, once again, be a familiar figure during services in Walton Church.

Colin wiped his eyes. He seemed to have recovered now. 'Goodness me – all this excitement's too much! Right, James. Didn't you mention some photos a while ago?'

'Oh, yes. Here they are.' James passed them round.

'These are good . . .' Colin said, leafing through them, 'especially these ones taken in the crypt.' He was studying one of the photos particularly closely. 'Wait a minute. Now that's really odd . . .'

'What is?' Lizzy asked.

She got no answer. Colin rose to his feet. 'Come with me, all of you,' he said excitedly. 'I want you to see this for yourselves.'

Colin unlocked the church door and led Mandy, James, Lizzy and Daniel down the steps to the crypt.

Mandy shivered. After the cosy kitchen the crypt was cold and gloomy. Colin didn't seem to notice. Torch in hand, he hurried straight over to the largest tomb, which was topped by a carving of the first vicar of Walton.

'Look at this,' Colin said. 'Have a good close look. Tell me what you see.'

Mandy and James looked at the stone carving.

'It's the first vicar of Walton,' James began, uncertainly. 'He's lying there with his hands together as if he's praying . . .'

'He's wearing a hooded robe,' Mandy added. 'And there's a sleeping cat curled up by his feet—' She stopped. There seemed something strangely familiar about that stone cat.

'Exactly! The cat!' Colin cried. 'That's it. Now – take a look at this!'

Lizzy came over to see for herself as Colin held up James's photo. The stern-faced first vicar of Walton was picked out in splendid detail: there were the folds in his robe, the beautifully carved hands . . . but there was no cat lying near his feet.

Mandy did a double-take. She ran her eyes down the photo again. No. She wasn't mistaken. 'Oh,' she said. 'But that's impossible. James – look. There's no cat in your photograph!'

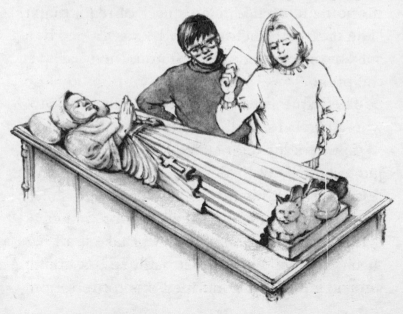

James frowned. He looked at the tomb, then back at his photo. 'I don't get it. What's going on?'

'You took your photos of the crypt the day before Bathsheba came back and led you to Daniel, didn't you, James?' Colin asked.

Mandy and James nodded.

'And who was Bathsheba running to when you saw her returning to the church?'

'The stone-coloured cat . . .' Mandy replied. Then she looked at the sleeping cat on top of the stone tomb and felt a shiver of realisation. 'The *stone* cat!' she whispered.

Everyone looked at the statue, then back at the photo.

'The stone cat brought Bathsheba back to where she belonged!' Mandy continued.

'To where she was needed. To save Daniel . . .' James added, awestruck.

Colin shook his head. 'It seems impossible. But I can't see any other explanation, either.'

Lizzy looked as if she couldn't take it all in. 'It's incredible,' she said. 'It really is. But would anyone mind if we continued this conversation in the kitchen? Daniel's getting a bit cold down here.'

'You go in, love,' Colin said. 'We'll follow you in a minute.'

'You know,' James said, going round the tomb to look at the first vicar of Walton's harsh face. 'I don't think this old chap was such an old misery, after all.'

'Why's that?' Mandy asked.

'Well, he was a cat-lover, wasn't he?'

Mandy and Colin laughed.

'That makes him OK in your book, does it?' Colin said with a wicked twinkle in his eye.

'Oh, yes,' Mandy said with feeling. 'All the best people love animals!'

'Seems like I'm off the hook too, then!' Colin laughed. 'Come on. Let's go back into the house. I think we all need a hot drink to warm us up.'

Colin made his way back towards the crypt steps. James followed him.

Mandy took one last look over her shoulder. 'Thank you for bringing Bathsheba back and saving Daniel,' she said softly to the sleeping stone cat. 'I'll probably never know where she's been – or how you did it . . . But thank you anyway.'

Somehow, Mandy knew for certain that no one would be seeing the mysterious stone-coloured cat around Walton churchyard again. Its task was done and it could once again rest between the feet of its beloved master.

As Mandy emerged from out of the crypt she glanced up to where Bathsheba's cat gargoyle was looking down. James and Colin came and stood beside her.

In the fading light, it almost looked as if the cat was smiling . . .

STALLION IN THE STORM
Animal Ark Hauntings 3

Lucy Daniels

Mandy and James will do anything to help an animal in distress. And sometimes even ghostly animals appear to need their help . . .

Mandy and James can hardly wait to accompany her dad to Folan's Racing Stables. But they find that Folan's is in trouble. Some of the jockeys believe it's because the stables are haunted by Tibor, one of their stallions, who died in a race. Can Mandy and James discover the truth – and help Tibor make his peace?

PONY IN THE POST
Animal Ark Christmas Special

Lucy Daniels

Mandy Hopes loves animals more than anything else. She knows quite a lot about them too: both her parents are vets and Mandy helps out in their surgery, Animal Ark.

A wrong delivery at Animal Ark brings a big surprise – the tiniest horse that Mandy has ever seen! The Miniature Horse was meant for Tania Benster, a newcomer to Welford. But Tania's parents have just divorced and she's too upset to care about her gift. Can Mandy show Tania how much this little horse has to offer?

CHINCHILLA UP THE CHIMNEY
Animal Ark 42

Lucy Daniels

Mandy Hope loves animals more than anything else. She knows quite a lot about them too: both her parents are vets and Mandy helps out in their surgery, Animal Ark.

When Animal Ark's receptionist, Jean Knox, returns from the shops, she brings back more than she'd bargained for: a chinchilla has crept in with her shopping! Before it can be caught it shoots off to hide. Mandy and James must find it – but there's no sign of the chinchilla anywhere!

ANIMAL ARK *by Lucy Daniels*

All Hodder Children's books are available at your local bookshop, or can be ordered direct from the publisher. Just tick the titles you would like and complete the details below. Prices and availability are subject to change without prior notice.

Please enclose a cheque or postal order made payable to *Bookpoint Ltd*, and send to: Hodder Children's Books, 39 Milton Park, Abingdon, OXON OX14 4TD, UK. Email Address: orders@bookpoint.co.uk

If you would prefer to pay by credit card, our call centre team would be delighted to take your order by telephone. Our direct line *01235 400414* (lines open 9.00 am–6.00 pm Monday to Saturday, 24 hour message answering service). Alternatively you can send a fax on *01235 400454*.

TITLE		FIRST NAME		SURNAME	

ADDRESS	
DAYTIME TEL:		POST CODE	

If you would prefer to pay by credit card, please complete: Please debit my Visa/Access/Diner's Card/American Express (delete as applicable) card no:

Signature ....

Expiry Date: ....

If you would NOT like to receive further information on our products please tick the box. ❏